A MAN CALLED LAWLESS

The promise of well-paid work draws the man called Lawless to Deming, New Mexico. But when he discovers the nature of the job, he decides to pass. Fate, however, has other ideas. Within minutes of his arrival in town, he is forced to kill three hired guns, putting him at odds with the local law. And when his would-be employer is kidnapped by Mexican bandits, Lawless has no choice but to cross the border and rescue her . . .

STEVE HAYES

A MAN
CALLED
LAWLESS

Complete and Unabridged

LINFORD
Leicester

First published in Great Britain in 2013 by
Sixgold

First Linford Edition
published 2014
by arrangement with
Steve Hayes and David Whitehead

A catalogue record for this book is available
from the British Library.

ISBN 978–1–4448–1959–5

Published by
F. A. Thorpe (Publishing)
Anstey, Leicestershire

Set by Words & Graphics Ltd.
Anstey, Leicestershire
Printed and bound in Great Britain by
T. J. International Ltd., Padstow, Cornwall

This book is printed on acid-free paper

For the Burger Night Guys

1

The stranger on the dust-caked, pure-bred Spanish stallion seemed unaware that he was riding against the flow of traffic that always cluttered Pine Street around noon.

A tall, straight-backed, raw-boned man wearing range clothes and a trail-soiled campaign hat, he ignored the shaking fists and angry shouts that oncoming drivers hurled at him as they swerved their wagons to avoid him, and went on checking the names on the storefronts and office windows lining both sides of the crowded street.

He was obviously looking for someone. Just as obviously he didn't seem to care how many people he inconvenienced in order to find them. Either that or, as some of the onlookers thought, he was too damned independent to give a hoot about such mundane conformity.

Yet, despite his apparent defiance and lack of consideration, he didn't look like a gunman on the prod or a belligerent bully who should be feared or avoided; on the contrary, below the brim of his old sweat-stained hat, passers-by saw a lean, cleft-chinned, pleasant face that needed shaving, light gray eyes full of whimsy and a generous mouth with laugh lines creasing the corners. The stranger also needed a haircut, his long dark hair curling over the collar of his rough-cut leather jacket. He was more rugged than handsome, yet the way the women eyed him as he rode past suggested here was a man who only slept alone by choice.

Halfway along the street he found the name he was looking for. Reining up, he dismounted and tied the pale gray stallion to the hitch-rail outside the office of: SAMUEL A. HERD — ATTORNEY AT LAW — DEMING, NEW MEXICO.

Immediately a small scruffy boy ran

up to him, grubby palm extended. 'Hey, mister, want for me to watch your horse?'

'Nope.'

'Only cost a nickel.'

'I said no.'

The boy stubbornly stood his ground. 'Be right sorry if he gets stoled.'

The stranger eyed the stallion as if still trying to figure the complex horse out. Physically, it was a head-turner. Strongly built, compact yet elegant, with a proud head and a flowing dark-gray mane and tail, it drew envious glances from anyone who appreciated fine horseflesh; but emotionally, the horse was a mess. It was high-strung, temperamental and unpredictable — all traits contrary to the breed, which was bred to be gentle, obedient and docile. Even now, as the stranger looked at the stallion it acted skittishly, tossing its head, chafing at the bit, nervously looking around as if it feared everything.

'What makes you think — ?' the

3

stranger began then stopped as a mongrel ran past, barking, causing the horse to dance sideward and jerk its head so that the reins snapped taut, threatening to jerk the hitch-rail loose. The stranger spoke soothingly to it in Spanish, trying to calm the stallion, and then spat the dust from his throat. ' — somebody's goin' to steal him?' he concluded.

The boy shrugged. 'Could happen, couldn't it?'

'Son,' the stranger said wryly, 'my luck ain't that good.' Pulling his Winchester '91 from its scabbard, he slapped the dust from his clothes with his hat and stepped onto the board-walk. As he reached the office door he paused and without turning, dug a coin from his pocket and flipped it over his shoulder to the disappointed boy.

Catching it, the boy saw it was a quarter. His eyes bugged. 'Hey, thanks, mister!' And he ran off before his benefactor could change his mind.

The stranger looked after the boy and

smiled, as if he saw a reflection of himself. Then he opened the door and stepped inside — bumping into a young woman who was leaving in a hurry.

'O-Oh!'

She would have fallen if he hadn't grabbed her. As it was he held her long enough to steady her then released her, stepped back and started to go around her.

Indignant, she blocked his path, saying: 'Least you could do is apologize.'

'For what?'

'Almost knocking me off my — ' She stopped and took another look at him. At once her annoyance was replaced by relief. 'Why you're him, aren't you?'

'Him?'

'Lawless — I mean, Mr. Lawless. You are, aren't you? Oh, please, tell me you are.'

'Why should you care who I am?'

'Because I . . . I've been waiting for you to get here, that's why.'

Lawless eyed the name on the door

5

before saying: 'You're Samuel Herd?'

'No-o, of course not,' she laughed. 'My name's Tess. Tess Albright. I'm the person you've come to see.'

Lawless frowned. ''fraid you got me mixed up with someone else, ma'am. I'm here to see Mr. Herd. And if you'll be kind enough to step aside — '

'I'll do better than that, Mr. Lawless. I'll take you to him.' Turning, she started along the narrow hallway of closed doors.

Lawless followed, shortening his normal long easy stride so that he didn't overtake her. That gave him time to size her up. From in front or behind she was easy on the eye. He judged she was on the good side of thirty. She looked slim and curvy in blue denim and boots, and her freckled but pretty face was framed by unruly, tawny curls. But what he liked most about her was her audaciousness — a kind of cheerful self-confidence that possessed no trace of arrogance. He liked the way she walked too. Not like one of those fancy, perfumed ladies from St. Louis or New Orleans, but like a young spring-born filly, striding with impatient energy that quickly brought them to the last office.

'Here we are,' she said, opening the door.

'Thanks.' He waited for her to leave.

'If you don't mind,' she said, not moving, 'I'll come in with you.'

'And if I do?'

Taken aback, she said: 'Then I'll wait in the outer office. But I don't know why you should. After all, I'm paying for all this.'

Lawless frowned, troubled by her remark, but didn't say anything.

Inside, the small reception office was fenced off by a low wooden railing with a swing-gate. A gray-haired, stern-faced, neatly dressed secretary sat filing papers at her desk. She looked up over the top of her spectacles as they entered and seemed puzzled to see Tess.

'Oh, dear me,' she said, her accent British. 'Did you forget something, Mrs. Albright?'

'Uh-uh. But guess who this is — our missing Mr. Lawless.'

The secretary, Miss Hobbs, eyed him sourly. 'Mr. Herd was expecting you two days ago.'

'Expectations,' Lawless drawled. 'Now there's a word that rolls easy off a lawyer's tongue.'

'I beg your pardon?'

'Course, I doubt if it'd mean much to the border trash who tried to kill me . . . or to the renegade Mescaleros who shot and ate my pack-horse, but it's still a truly fine word.' He smiled sweetly at Miss Hobbs, who'd turned pale.

'I-I'll go t-tell Mr. Herd you're here,' she stammered. Jumping up, she hurried to the office door behind her, knocked, and entered.

'Shame on you, Mr. Lawless,' Tess said, chuckling. 'Making up an awful story like that. You scared the poor woman to death.'

'Who says I made it up?' He winked as he spoke and Tess sensed he was

8

teasing her but couldn't be sure.

Before she could respond, Miss Hobbs reappeared and beckoned to Lawless. 'Mr. Herd will see you now, sir.' She stepped back so he could walk past her into the office, then shut the door and returned to her desk.

'What a beastly, vulgar man,' she said, shuffling her papers. 'As if anyone, even an Apache, would eat a horse.'

Tess started to say that Apaches had no regard for horses, often riding them until they dropped and then eating them, but not wanting to upset the secretary any further, said instead: 'I'm sure he was just joking, Louise.'

'Perhaps,' Miss Hobbs said huffily. 'But I hardly find that a subject to joke about — ' She paused as the office door opened and Samuel Herd beckoned to Tess. 'Please, come in, Mrs. Albright.'

Tess rose and entered the office.

Herd, a large silver-haired man in a black suit, stiff-collared white shirt and red bow-tie, closed the door and pulled up a chair before his desk so she could sit beside Lawless. Then returning behind his desk, he said: 'I've explained to Mr. Lawless that this is your war party, so I thought it would be faster all around if you heard what he had to say first-hand.'

'Thank you, Arthur. I appreciate that.'

The lawyer opened a file on the desk before him, saying: 'All right then, to business.' Taking out a photograph, he gave it to Lawless. 'This is Mrs. Albright's husband, Tucker.' He waited for Lawless to take a good look at the photo before adding: 'He was kidnapped nine — no, ten days ago while in Mexico.'

'Where in Mexico?'

'Chihuahua,' Tess said. 'Palomas to be exact.'

'What was he doin' in that hellhole?'

There was a brief awkward pause in which Herd looked uneasily at Tess.

'Conducting business,' he said finally.

'What kind of business?'

'I fail to see why that's any of your — '

'Arthur, answer him, please.'

The lawyer gruffly cleared his throat. 'I . . . uh . . . we believe it was his intention to buy more land from one of the rancheros. The Albright ranch, in case you don't know, borders Mexico and — '

Tess stopped him. 'Arthur,' she said firmly. 'If Mr. Lawless is to help us, I will not start out by lying to him. My husband,' she said, turning to Lawless, 'goes there frequently.'

'Why?'

'Is that important?'

'Won't know till you tell me.'

'Very well. In his own words — to amuse himself.'

'In what way?'

Tess hesitated, blushed, then swallowed her pride and said: 'He finds the local women — how shall I say — *entertaining*.'

'Uh-*huh* . . . '

There was disappointment in his

tone and Tess felt stung by it.

'You're wondering why I put up with his — uh — philandering?'

'What you do or don't do, ma'am, is none of my business.'

'Come now,' she said reproachfully. 'I was truthful with you. The least you could do is respond in kind.'

Lawless shrugged. 'Did cross my mind.'

'Mrs. Albright,' Herd said sharply. 'Mr. Lawless is being paid to *find* your husband, not judge him or his dalliances.'

'Oh, for heaven's sake, Arthur!' Tess exclaimed. 'Stop trying to protect a reputation that was tarnished long before I even met him.' Turning to Lawless, she added: 'I knew what I was getting into when I married Tuck — was warned about it by almost everyone, including his own father. But I was so desperately in love with him that I — well, let's just say I thought I could change him.' She laughed sourly. 'Isn't that what all women think when they marry a Don Juan — that her love is so special she can change him — keep him satisfied?'

Her resigned bitterness made Lawless feel uncomfortable and for several moments he didn't answer.

Finally he said: 'Any idea why your husband was kidnapped?'

'If you mean, were any of Tuck's lady friends involved — I don't know.'

'How about the ransom note — what did it say?'

Herd gruffly cleared his throat. 'There was no ransom note.'

'Then how do you know he was kidnapped?'

'Someone told Mrs. Albright.'

'A drifter,' Tess said as Lawless turned to her. 'He'd just ridden up from Palomas and heard I was worried about Tuck, who hadn't come home like he always does, and said — '

'For fifty pesos he'd tell you what'd happened to him?'

'Y-Yes. How'd you know?'

'It's the goin' rate for wives with

13

missing husbands,' Lawless said.

'Damn you, sir,' exclaimed Herd. 'How dare you talk to Mrs. Albright like that!'

Lawless ignored him and said to Tess: 'This drifter. After you'd paid him what'd he tell you?'

'That as he was leaving Palomas, he saw some bandits riding off with my husband.'

'Bandits?'

'Yes. *Montana bandidos*, he called them.'

'What would mountain bandits want with your husband?'

'I've no idea, Mr. Lawless.'

'But you're sure that's what the drifter said?'

'Positive.'

'Mrs. Albright speaks Spanish fluently,' broke in Herd. 'So she — '

Lawless cut him off, saying: 'Well, least you had brains enough not to ride down there yourself.' Then as he read her reaction: 'Oh, Sweet Judas, you didn't!'

14

'What would you have done, Mr. Lawless — if you'd been in my shoes?'

'You comparin' yourself to me?'

'Course not. I'm just asking you what — '

'Had a lot of experience dealin' with bandits, have you?'

'No, but I thought — *hoped* that the man might be mistaken.'

'And if he had been?'

'What do you mean?'

'I mean, Mrs. Albright, exactly what did you intend to do *if* and *when* you found your husband — shoot him or beg him to come home?'

Tess stiffened as if slapped. 'You don't have to be rude, Mr. Lawless. I'm well aware of how stupid I appear without having you rub it in. Unfortunately, loving my husband as much as I do, I sometimes don't make the best choices.'

Lawless didn't say anything. Foolish and impetuous as this blue-eyed woman was, he couldn't help but admire her honesty and courage

15

— even if, by the sound of it, they were sadly misplaced.

'So, will you help me find him?' Tess asked hopefully.

'Sorry.' Lawless got to his feet, towering over her. 'But I wish you luck.'

'Wait — ' Tess grasped his arm. 'Would you tell me why not?'

'I've had my fill of Mexico.'

'But that's exactly why I had Arthur send for you.'

'Ma'am?'

'Arthur wired your friend, Marshal Macahan in El Paso. He said you used to live there. Says you know the country better than most and that if anyone can find Tuck, you can.'

Lawless looked uncomfortable. 'Well, now, Ezra's a good man an' I'd be the last person to question his judgment, but he does tend to exaggerate some.'

'Look, if it's a matter of money — '

'It ain't.'

'I'd be willing to pay whatever you ask,' Tess said as if he hadn't spoken.

'I said — it's not money.'

16

'What, then? Why won't you help me?'

Again, he didn't answer.

'Tell me . . . please.'

Lawless sighed, knowing he was about to hurt her. ''cause it would be a pure waste of my time.'

'In other words, you think my husband's dead?'

Lawless tugged on the lobe of his ear, something he did when he didn't want to answer someone's question.

Tess refused to let him off the hook. 'Is that a hunch, or a conclusion based on personal experience?'

Lawless sighed. 'Here's the short of it, Mrs. Albright. If *bandidos* did kidnap your husband and haven't demanded any ransom, then they just wanted to rob him. And if I'm right, then yes, that means he's already dead.'

Tess swallowed hard, but refused to admit defeat.

'You may be right,' she admitted. 'I won't deny that I haven't considered that myself. But Tuck is my husband,

and woeful husband that he may be I could never live with myself if I didn't do everything in my power to find him.' Turning to her lawyer, she said: 'Make sure Mr. Lawless gets his travel fee, Arthur.'

He nodded glumly.

'Thank you for coming,' Tess said to Lawless. 'I'm sorry things didn't work out.' She spun around before he could see her deep disappointment and hurried from the office.

Lawless looked admiringly after her. 'Fine spirited woman.'

'Yet you won't help her?'

'True.'

'Well, I'm sure you have your reasons. Here ... ' Herd finished signing a check, tore it out of the book and handed it to Lawless. 'Take this to the bank. They'll give you your money.'

'Keep it,' Lawless said. 'It was time I put some dust between me and El Paso anyway.' He left the office before the surprised lawyer could say anything.

2

Once outside Lawless jammed his hat on and pulled the brim down low to shield his eyes from the glaring hot sun. He paused there a moment on the sunbaked boardwalk, visualizing the young and vibrant Albright woman and wishing he could have helped her.

But he couldn't — not unless he was willing to die for her; and he wasn't. Admittedly, the ten thousand dollars she was offering to anyone who could rescue her husband was tempting, but what good was money to him if he was dead? And if he ever did return to Mexico, there was no doubt in his mind that he would be gunned down.

Shrugging off his frustration, he started toward his horse. His long moving shadow reached the jittery stallion first, causing it to nicker and shy nervously.

'Calm down, dammit,' Lawless told the animal. 'Don't go gettin' spooked on account of a stupid shadow — ' He broke off as beyond the stallion, in the middle of the street, he saw three hard-faced men walking toward him.

They weren't the only men crossing the busy street, and he only caught a glimpse of them before a passing freight wagon hid them from his sight. But he instantly sensed their menace and knew instinctively they were gunmen and that they were coming for him.

The wagon lumbered on its way and the gunmen reappeared. As if to prove Lawless right, the man in the middle thumbed back the hammers of his shotgun and raised it, intending to blast away.

Lawless was too quick for him. Throwing himself flat, he rolled off the boardwalk onto the dirt under a parked buckboard. From there he quickly levered a round into his rifle and fired at the gunman.

The bullet punched a hole in the

man's chest. He staggered and dropped to his knees, shocked as he saw blood reddening his shirt, then fell forward. Dead.

In the next few moments several things happened almost at once.

Startled by the gunshot, the stallion whinnied shrilly, rearing up with such force that it jerked the hitch-rail loose. The panicked horse pawed at the air, the broken piece of wood flailing at the end of the reins adding to its terror —

The other two gunmen jumped back, avoiding the stallion's hoofs, and grabbed their six-guns —

Everyone within earshot stopped, alarmed, then ran for cover —

Lawless, meanwhile, fired another shot from under the wagon —

The bullet hit the nearest gunman in the thigh. Yelping, he grabbed his wounded leg, hopped around for a moment then lost his balance and went down —

Lawless snapped off a third round, ending the man's life —

The last gunman, realizing where the shots had come from, hunkered down in an effort to see where Lawless was hiding —

Lawless shot him in the face, sending him sprawling backward.

It was over in less than ten seconds.

Three men lay dead in the street.

None of the frightened, scattered onlookers moved.

The ensuing silence seemed louder than the shooting.

Then, gradually, people cowering on the boardwalk and behind cover began to cautiously reappear as they realized the gunfight had ended.

Lawless got to his feet, rifle at the ready, and approached the dead gunmen.

A gun cocked behind him. 'Hold it right there, mister.'

Lawless froze.

'Drop that long gun.'

Lawless obeyed and heard someone step off the boardwalk and come up behind him. Hands half-raised, he slowly turned and saw Sheriff Skye

Woodson approaching, six-gun leveled at Lawless's belly.

'It was self-defense, sheriff. Ask anyone.'

'Don't have to. Saw the whole thing from start to finish.'

'Then — ?'

'Keep them hands where they are,' warned the old weathered lawman, 'an' give me your iron. And do it real slow.'

Lawless handed over his Colt .45 and the sheriff tucked it in his belt before saying: 'Self-defense or not, mister, there's been a killin' — three killings to be exact, an' you're gonna have to cool your heels for a spell until I can find out more about what went on.'

'You arrestin' me?'

'Detaining you.'

'In jail?'

'Till I corral all the facts, yeah.' The sheriff eyed the three corpses. 'Know any of these men?'

'No. But I know who sent 'em.'

'Who?'

'Man I once worked for.'

'A name would help.'

'Señor Vargas.'

'Don Aldonza Vargas — governor of Chihuahua?'

'The same.'

Sheriff Woodson whistled softly. 'Well, I don't know what you done to make him sore, mister, but whatever it was I hope it was worth it — 'cause if he's sendin' gunmen up here to kill you, your future's shorter than a dead rose. C'mon,' he nodded for Lawless to follow him.

'First, I need to put up my horse.'

'I'll have one of my deputies do it. Livery's just down the street. Where is he?'

Lawless thumbed at the stallion. 'The gray there.'

The sheriff looked at the elegant Spanish purebred, then at Lawless, and frowned. 'I don't want to seem rude, mister, but — '

'What's a saddle stiff like me doin' with a horse like that?'

'Sounds like you been asked that before?'

'More times than I like, yeah.'

'Is that what this trouble's about — you ridin' off with one of Governor Vargas's prize stallions?'

'I didn't steal him if that's what you mean. He was a gift.'

The sheriff grunted wryly. 'Seems like the governor's changed his mind.'

'Vargas didn't give me the horse. His daughter, Delfina, did.'

The lawman's bristly gray eyebrows raised questioningly but he didn't say anything.

'As for havin' one of your deputies stable my horse,' Lawless continued, 'make sure he ain't married — else there's goin' to be another widow in town.' Then as the sheriff frowned: 'Got my word I won't ride out on you.'

The old lawman studied Lawless for a long, hard moment, then sighed as if he'd just inherited trouble. 'I'll be waitin' for you in my office. Don't disappoint me.'

3

McCanty's Livery was owned by a tiny, cranky old Scotsman who loved horses but had little use for humans.

One of the first pioneers to settle in Deming — so named for Mary Ann Deming Crocker, the wife of railroad magnate Charles Crocker — he'd lost his wife to typhoid fever shortly after opening the livery. He'd never remarried and from then on he'd become more and more bitter.

Now, as Lawless led the stallion into the livery, the hostler stopped tossing fresh hay into one of the stalls, turned, leaned on his pitchfork and eyed the tall stranger. But only for a moment. Then his gaze settled on the Spanish stallion and his whole demeanor changed for the good.

'What canna do for ye?' he asked Lawless, his eyes appraising every inch of the pale gray horse.

'Grain an' stall him overnight.'

'Cost ye two dollars.'

Lawless dug a handful of coins out of his jeans. 'You take pesos?'

'Laddie, do I look like a Mex' to you?'

'Cool your water, old-timer.' Lawless found two silver dollars and handed them to the hostler. 'Maybe I should stall him. He can be a handful.'

'Day I canna do my job's the day they bury me toes up.'

'Suit yourself.' Lawless handed the reins to the little old Scotsman and turned to leave. 'Oh, yeah, an' he gets spooked by his own shadow.'

'Don't we all,' McCanty said. He faced the stallion, no taller than the horse's withers, and gently rubbed the soft gray muzzle. 'Aye, now, but you're a right bonnie lad.'

Lawless started to warn the hostler about getting bitten, then stopped and watched in surprised silence as the old Scotsman led the now-placid stallion toward the stall he'd just cleaned out. 'What's he answer to?' he asked, looking back at Lawless.

'Alano. Means — '

'I know what it means.' McCanty looked admiringly at the stallion, then nodded. 'Fits.'

Lawless waited there long enough to make sure the hostler got the stallion safely into the stall, then turned and walked out.

When he entered the sheriff's office a few minutes later, he got another surprise: seated across the desk from the lawman, waiting for him, was the lawyer, Arthur Herd.

'Mrs. Albright asked me to represent you,' he told Lawless.

'I told him you didn't need no shingle mouthpiece,' Sheriff Woodson said as Lawless looked at him. 'But seems he don't believe me.'

'Why should I?' Herd demanded. 'Almost the whole town saw that trash start shooting at my client — yet you still insist on keeping him locked up like a common drunk.'

'First of all,' the sheriff said, 'like I told him, it's only till I sort things out. An' second of all, that ain't how it happened. Saw it with my own eyes. This fella shot first an' then killed all three — ain't that right, mister?' he said to Lawless.

'If you saw it,' Lawless replied, 'then you know I had no choice. Fella I gunned down was aiming to blow a hole through my belly with a scattergun.'

'That's what all the witnesses I spoke to said,' put in Herd. 'Said my client would've been splashed all over the boardwalk if he hadn't fired when he did.'

The sheriff sighed, heaved his shoulders and made a decision. 'If I let you spend the night at the Baker Hotel, does that word you give me earlier still hold?'

Lawless nodded.

'Then we'll talk in the mornin'.'

'How 'bout my pistol and saddle gun?'

'They stay with me.'

'What if Vargas sent more than three men?'

'Try not to let 'em find you till mornin'.'

'You're a hard man, sheriff.'

'No, son. A hard man would be talkin' to you through bars.'

'C'mon, Lawless,' Herd said, rising, 'supper's on me.'

They ate outside at a plank table under an awning at *El Rosarita*, a cantina across from the Baker Hotel. It was getting dark and a breeze off the *Tres Hermanas*, three sharply pointed mountains just south of the city, had turned the evening cool.

Lawless was hungrier than he'd realized. He ate a big bowl of beef, beans and rice, sopped up every last morsel with fresh-made corn tortillas and then washed everything down with a tall frothy beer.

Across from him Herd, a big eater himself, wolfed down a double serving of chilli and beans and afterward sat there, leaning back from the table, hands clasped across his belly, contentedly smoking a Mexican cigar and farting away his gas.

'I wired Marshal Macahan,' he said, watching Lawless roll a smoke, 'asking for a personal reference. You know, just in case we have to go to court.'

'Reckon it'll go that far?'

'Uh-uh. But it's always nice to have an ace up your sleeve.'

'Macahan ever get back to you?'

'Sure.' Herd blew a smoke ring before adding: 'Said he wished his two brothers were half the man you are.'

Lawless chuckled. 'Like I told Mrs. Albright, Ezra tends to exaggerate.'

'I also wired an important judge I know in Mexico City.'

Lawless flared a match on the table and lit his hand-rolled. 'And?'

'He presented a somewhat different picture of you.'

'Can't wait to hear it.'

Herd paused to spit out a flake of tobacco. 'Seems you have quite a reputation as a *pistolero*, Mr. Lawless.'

'I did what Governor Vargas paid me to do.'

'With great gusto, apparently.'

'I didn't enjoy killing if that's what you're insinuatin'.'

'Didn't shy away from it either.'

'It was them or me.'

'And one way or another you made sure it was always them, didn't you?'

Lawless stiffened and his eyes went hard. 'If something's chewin' at you, lawyer man, spit it out.'

'Well, I was just thinking . . . obviously, you're very fast with a gun.'

'But?'

'Surely one of all the men you faced was faster?'

'More than one. Just not as accurate.'

'Or maybe they didn't see you coming.'

'Some men would kill you for what you're implying.'

'Lucky for me you're not one of them.'

Lawless eyed Herd through exhaled smoke. 'I never shot a man whose eyes I couldn't see.'

'I believe you. But for the record, Lawless, it wouldn't matter to me even if you had.'

'That's 'cause you kill folks with words, not lead.'

Herd chuckled and tapped the ash from his cigar. 'If you're trying to insult my manhood, sir, save your breath. In my opinion integrity and morality are misplaced in today's world — 'specially in a wild, corrupt country like Mexico where everything is for the taking . . . women included.'

Lawless whitened and instinctively reached for his Colt — only to find the holster empty.

'Must be your lucky day, lawyer man.'

Unfazed, Herd blew the ash from his cigar tip. 'Come now, Mr. Lawless, no need to get salty. I meant no offense. We're both grown men. And we both take what we want, don't we?'

'I didn't 'take' the governor's daughter. I didn't even ask Delfina to run off with me. That was all her idea.'

'So Judge Garcia said. But apparently, the young lady neglected to mention this to her father — who was quite upset, to say the least, when he discovered his only daughter intended to marry a *gringo* — a *gringo* that some say he once loved like a son.'

Lawless fought down his anger and drained his beer before asking: 'There a point to all this?'

'The point, *amigo*, is that I'd like you to reconsider Mrs. Albright's offer.'

Lawless suddenly reached across the table, grabbed the lawyer by the shirt front and jerked him up out of his chair.

'I ain't your *amigo*,' he said softly. 'Not now, not ever. Clear?'

'S-Sure.'

Lawless released the startled lawyer, who slumped back down in his chair.

'As for Mrs. Albright, I've changed my mind. I've decided to help her find her husband.'

'You have? Why, that's wonderful. I'll tell her as soon as I get back to the hotel.'

'You can also tell her that I want half my money up front.'

'No problem. That was her intention anyway. In fact, meet me at the First National Bank in the morning — ten o'clock, say — and I'll have them pay you right there and then.'

'I'll be there.' Lawless got to his feet, taller even than the big fleshy lawyer, and dug out some loose change.

'Put it away,' Herd told him. 'Supper's on me, remember?'

Ignoring him, Lawless dropped the coins on the table and walked off.

Herd watched him go with an amused sneer.

4

Early the next morning Lawless entered the sheriff's office and found his deputy, Gifford Hanks, dozing with his muddy boots propped up on the old lawman's desk.

There was something irreverent about the sight and it pissed Lawless off. He knocked the deputy's legs off the desk, startling the scrawny young man so that he almost fell out of the chair.

'W-Wha — the — hell,' he exclaimed; then on recognizing Lawless and seeing the tall man's grim, tight-lipped expression, he decided not to yell at him and instead muttered something about some folks having no respect for the law.

'I respect the law,' Lawless said. 'An' believe me, sonny, you ain't it. Now, where's your boss?'

'Had to ride over to Las Cruces — left afore sunup.'

'He leave any instructions for me?'

'Just said I was to give you your guns and tell you not to be here when he got back.'

'So give 'em to me.'

The deputy took Lawless's Colt .45 out of the desk drawer and his rifle from the gun-rack on the wall, and handed them to him. Lawless checked both weapons to make sure they were loaded, holstered his six-gun and then turned to leave.

'Oh, and he told me to tell you not to drag your feet about doin' it.'

'No, he didn't,' Lawless said. 'That's your mouth workin', sonny, and if I was you I'd keep it shut till your brains can catch up — if they ever do, which ain't likely.' He walked out, door slamming behind him.

The First National Bank was an impressive building opposite the yellow-and-brown railroad depot. Lawless dismounted outside the entrance, hitched the stallion to the tie-rail and entered the bank.

There were two men at the teller window, but neither of them was Samuel Herd. Lawless looked at the clock on the wall. It was a few minutes after ten. About to sit on the waiting bench, he paused as he heard someone enter. Turning, he expected to see the lawyer — and instead found himself facing Tess Albright.

''Morning, Mr. Lawless . . . ' She approached, smiling, dressed in expensive riding clothes, hand-tooled boots and a man's wide-brimmed, flat-crowned hat. 'I hope you slept well.'

'Well enough, ma'am.'

'Mr. Herd won't be coming,' she said as his gaze wandered to the door. 'I'm here to give you your money person-ally.'

''preciate that.'

'Afterwards,' she added, moving to the open teller window, 'we'll get the pack horse from the livery then go to

Hart's Mercantile and pick up our supplies.'

Lawless stopped in mid-step, saying: "Our' supplies, ma'am?'

'Of course. I'm going with you.' Seeing his surprise, she quickly added: 'Didn't Mr. Herd mention that I'd be accompanying you last night at supper?'

'No, ma'am.'

'That's odd. I expressly told him to — '

'If he had, Mrs. Albright, I never would've agreed to go.'

Now it was her turn to be surprised. 'Why on earth not?'

'If you don't know, reckon I can't explain it.'

'Try.'

Lawless tugged on his ear lobe, but didn't respond.

'You disappoint me, Mr. Lawless.'

'Not the first woman to say that.'

Tess sighed and shook her head. 'I thought you were different — special.'

'Ma'am?'

'That you were man enough not to

feel threatened by a woman's presence.'

He felt verbally slapped and yet knew that any response he made would only get him into an argument he couldn't win.

'Is there anything I can say to make you change your mind, Mr. Lawless?'

'Reckon not.'

Tess sighed again. 'Very well. Then I'll just have to hire someone else or go alone. Good day, Mr. Lawless.' She was gone before he could say anything.

He went to the window and looked through the bars. Outside, Tess untied her sorrel, swung up into the saddle in one smooth graceful motion, and rode off.

Lawless knew he should have felt relieved, but instead he wanted to kick himself.

5

Ravenous, he stayed in town long
enough to enjoy a platter of ham and
eggs and a stack of hotcakes, then
finished his third cup of coffee, paid his
check and left the cantina.

Outside it was already hot. There
was no wind, which was unusual, and a
host of flies buzzed around the pale
gray stallion that was tied up outside.
Flicking them away with its tail, the
Spanish purebred stamped its feet and
snorted angrily as the tall man
approached.

'Quit fussin',' Lawless said, untying
the horse and stepping up into the
saddle. 'We're headed for the high
country. No flies up there to bother
you.' He nudged the stallion with his
spurs and the high-spirited horse
broke into an immediate prancing trot
that would have become a gallop if

Lawless hadn't pulled back on the reins, murmuring: 'Easy, *hombre* . . . easy . . . '

He turned at the corner and started down Front Street. Wagons, buckboards and riders moved along the street and the boardwalks were busy with towns-people going about their business.

Ahead, on his left, Lawless saw a crowd of men and women gathered about a lone packhorse that was loaded down with supplies. It was caked with sweat and trail dust and as Lawless drew closer he recognized Deputy Gifford Hanks among the crowd. The scrawny deputy was having a heated conversation with Samuel Herd, who seemed very upset about something.

On seeing Lawless approaching Herd waved at him, yelling: 'Wait! Hold up, Lawless!'

Lawless reined in the stallion and waited for Herd to push through the crowd up to him.

'*Que pasa?*'

'It's Mrs. Albright,' Herd exclaimed.

'She's missing — possibly abducted.'

Something clammy dropped in Lawless's stomach. 'That hers?' he pointed to the packhorse.

'Yes. One of Doc Evans's sons, Matt, found it wandering along the Deming Road not far from the border. Knowing it belonged to Mrs. Albright, he looked around but couldn't find her or any tracks that might have been hers. He did find this though,' he lifted up Tess's wide-brimmed, flat-crowned Stetson, 'lying in the dirt beside the trail.'

Lawless frowned, concerned. 'What about her horse?'

'No sign of it. But he did find a bunch of other tracks,' Herd added. ''As if several horses had been milling around,' was how he put it.'

'They lead anywhere?'

'To the border, he said, where they crossed over into Mexico. Matt didn't go any farther, but he did talk to some of the villagers in Columbus, who claimed they hadn't seen Mrs. Albright or any riders. As a last resort, Matt spoke to an old prospector named Flapjack Joe, who'd come to town for supplies. Admittedly he's not the most reliable source alive, but Matt said the old man swore up and down that he'd seen a woman fitting Mrs. Albright's description riding with a dozen or so Mexicans — '

'*Bandidos*?'

'Flapjack didn't say that but from his description of them, Matt's sure they were.'

'Did this Flapjack fella mention if she was a prisoner, or goin' willingly?'

'Uh-uh. But he did say she wasn't trying to escape. But then, why would she? I mean what would be the point? They'd only ride her down or, worse, shoot her.'

Mind churning, Lawless didn't say anything for several moments. 'What're you goin' to do about it?' he asked then.

'Try and find her of course. I've already wired Skye — Sheriff Woodson in Las Cruces and he gave me the authority — well, he actually gave

Deputy Hanks the authority, but that drink of water's as useless as tits on a steer — to round up a posse and meet him at Columbus.'

'Then, what?'

'That'd be up to Skye. But, truth is, I doubt if he'd take it upon himself to cross into Mexico. He's got no legal authority there and besides, even if he had, he'd only butt heads with the *rurales* and sure as hell that'd end up in gunplay.'

'Then what's the point of him meetin' you there?'

'Have to ask him that,' Herd said. 'Maybe he's got friends or contacts there, and plans on enlisting their help to find Mrs. Albright.'

Lawless grunted, displeased. Troubled by the ugly pictures that his mind was conjuring up, he said: 'I'll be ridin' with you to Columbus.'

Herd shot him a withering look. 'Little late for redemption, isn't it?'

'I hope not. But I'll tell you this,' Lawless added grimly, 'unlike Sheriff

Woodson I won't be stopped on 'count of the border. I'll follow those bastards until I find Mrs. Albright an' then bring her back — even if I have to kill 'em wholesale to do it.'

'Fair enough,' Herd said. 'Let's just hope by that time Tess isn't a corpse.'

The Old Deming Road, originally a wagon trail, connected Deming to the tiny village of Columbus and, three miles beyond, the Mexican border.

Presently nothing more than a dusty eyesore in the hot desert scrubland, Columbus became nationally known years later when on March 9th, 1916, Pancho Villa's troops staged what would be the last attack by foreign forces on American soil.

Now, as Lawless rode alongside Herd at the head of a small, well-armed posse, he wasn't thinking about Pancho Villa, who hadn't become famous yet; his only concern was for Tess Albright. Though he owed her nothing, he couldn't help feeling partly responsible for her capture. Hell, if he hadn't refused to accompany her to Mexico, perhaps his presence and gunplay could have prevented it. And though it was too late to worry about that now, he couldn't completely ignore the guilt he felt deep down, and it made him all the more determined to rescue her.

The posse continued to ride south-ward. Dusk was approaching and in the violet half-light he could see the three sharp-pointed peaks of the *Tres Hermanas* on his right. Soon after that they came within sight of Columbus, a scattering of wood-frame shacks, adobe buildings and cantinas separated by rutted dirt streets.

There was no law in Columbus: disagreements were settled by fists or guns. Lawless knew the place well, having ridden through the village several times while working for Governor Vargas, either on his way out of or into Mexico. On one of those occasions he'd been forced into a gunfight by two gunmen out to avenge the death of their brother, a belligerent drunk whom

Lawless had killed in Palomas. He'd tried to convince the gunmen that their brother had started the fight, but they wouldn't believe him and jerked their guns. Lawless shot them both before they cleared leather and now, as he and Herd led the posse past the small yellow adobe jail, he kept a wary eye on the riff-raff loitering outside the local cantinas in case there were any more Kingsley brothers seeking revenge.

The posse continued on along the main street, a former wagon trail that once it left town eventually led east to El Paso. Ahead on their left was *La Rosa*, an old pink cantina that catered to Americans and Mexicans who constantly crossed back and forth across the border. It was here they intended to rendezvous with Sheriff Woodson. Lawless saw several pack-mules and burros tied up outside, but no horses. He knew then that the sheriff hadn't arrived yet and turning to Herd, said:

'Be leavin' you now.'

The lawyer reined up, surprised. 'What d'you mean?'

'I'm headin' across the border.'

'By your lonesome?'

Lawless nodded. 'I know someone in Palomas who might help me find Mrs. Albright an' the sooner I get started the better.'

Herd studied him, trying to read his expression, then said: 'You're a hard man to figure, Lawless.'

'Not so hard.'

'I wouldn't have pegged you for a conscience.'

'You would've been right.'

'Really? What other reason would you risk getting killed for?'

'Reckon it's time I settled an old score.'

'Governor Vargas?'

Lawless let the question hang there, unanswered, for a moment; then he swung his horse around. '*Adios*, lawyer man.' He kicked the high-strung stallion into a mile-consuming lope and headed for the border.

6

Once he'd crossed over into Mexico, Lawless elevated his survival instincts to an acute level. Though it wasn't noticeable to anyone else, he became a coiled spring, ready to defend himself against any kind of danger. His brain never relaxed; his eyes never stopped moving. Every rock, bush and cactus became a potential hiding place for his enemies; every sound a possible threat to his life.

Keeping the skittish stallion moving at an easy lope across the flat desert scrubland, he soon reached Palomas, a dusty sunbaked *pueblo* that was a haven for outlaws, gunmen and border trash. Like with Columbus and all the other border towns, Lawless had been a frequent visitor while he was the governor's hired gun. During those visits he'd made countless enemies and only one friend, the owner of *El Tecalote* cantina, Angel Ortega.

Now, as he entered town, Lawless slowed the stallion to a walk and followed a narrow dirt street that ran between rows of squalid little adobe hovels, past a white church that faced the plaza, and eventually led to the main street that was lined with sun-scorched stores, cantinas and run-down multi-level dwellings.

El Tecalote was on a corner, next to an alley halfway along the street. Its white-washed walls had been chipped over the years by stray bullets, the striped awning over the patio was torn in place by endless winds and the picture of a gray owl over the entrance needed repainting.

But for Lawless it was the only sanctuary in Palomas, and as he dismounted and tied up the stallion for the first time since entering Mexico he felt welcome. Taking his rifle from its scabbard, he avoided the stallion's attempt to bite him — 'Damn you!

Keep your teeth to yourself' — and warily looked about him. Dusk had turned to darkness, sending most of the townspeople scurrying home. There were a few riders coming and going along the street, but upon sizing them up, Lawless decided none of them posed a threat. He turned back to the cantina. Lights burned in the windows and raucous laughter mingled with mariachi music could be heard inside.

Lawless listened for a few moments to see if he could identify any of the voices. He couldn't. Nor could he identify any of the horses tied to the hitch-rail. But knowing Governor Vargas had put a price on his head, he checked all the brands. He didn't recognize any of them. But he did notice that all the saddles were western, not the fancy Mexican *Charro* saddles that the governor insisted his men use, and that gave him some comfort. But he hadn't stayed alive all these years by taking risks or chances, so levering a round into his Winchester he made his way along the alley, around in back of the cantina and entered by the kitchen door.

Inside, the kitchen smelled of rural Mexican cooking — beans, chilli, onions, tortilla soup and tamales. Lawless stood in the doorway, the heat from the two wood-burning ovens greeting him like a warm caress, and watched as the Ortega women — mother Cecile and daughters Carmen, Consuelo and Clarissa — busied themselves with the cooking.

Suddenly the youngest, Clarissa, saw him standing there and squealed with delight. 'Señor Lawless,' she cried, waving her flour-whitened hands, 'is it really you?'

'It's me all right,' Lawless said, grinning. 'But can that truly be you, Clarissa — a beautiful young woman all grown up since I last saw you?'

Clarissa ran giggling to him, into his outstretched arms, hugging him and saying, 'Momma, Momma, look, it is Señor Lawless!'

'I see him, child,' her mother said. Then to her other daughters, who had stopped working to smile and flutter their eyelashes at Lawless: 'Both of you — back to work. You think those tortillas will cook themselves? *Prisa! Prisa!*'

'But we have not seen Señor Lawless for over a year,' the oldest, Consuelo, complained. 'Surely Papa would think us most rude if we did not welcome his dear friend properly.'

Cecile, knowing she was trapped, rolled her eyes, saying: 'Oh, very well. Get your greetings over with and then back to work with you. Hurry! Hurry!' she added as her daughters paused to primp their hair and straighten their dresses. 'We have customers to serve. Hungry customers! And I'm sure they do not care if you welcome Señor Lawless or not.'

Lawless extended his arms even wider and embraced all three teenagers, who could barely contain their excitement at seeing him. Looking over their heads at their mother, he mouthed 'Sorry,' to her and then grinned as she chidingly shook her head at him.

'Next time, señor,' she said, 'it will please me greatly if you plan your visit at some other time than dinner.' Her tone was scolding but the warm smile in her dark brown eyes told Lawless that she was as pleased to see him as her daughters.

'I'll keep that in mind, señora,' he replied, straight-faced. 'Now, if you'll tell me where your husband is, I'll let you get back to work.'

'Angel is where he always is,' Cecile said, ' — behind the bar.'

'Let me go, girls,' Lawless told the sisters. 'I got to talk to your father.'

'Do as he says,' insisted their mother when her daughters didn't obey. '*Pronto! Pronto!*'

'Aww, Momma,' Carmen began.

'Now!' her mother ordered. 'Or this frying pan will sting your behinds.'

Grudgingly, the sisters released Lawless and returned to work.

'You will stay for supper?' Cecile said to Lawless.

He grinned, 'Try an' stop me,' he said, and pushed out through the door.

7

Angel Ortega was delighted to see Lawless. Embracing his old friend, he told his son, Jorge, to take over the bar and led Lawless out on the patio. He brought along two glasses, limes, salt and a bottle of tequila and they toasted each other and reminisced for a while before Lawless came to the point and explained why he was there.

Ortega listened intently, remaining silent until Lawless had finished. Then he sadly shook his head and said that he'd heard nothing about a *gringo* woman being kidnapped by *bandidos*. In fact, he added, lately bandits had caused very little trouble on either side of the border, though rumors suggested President Diaz's government was in turmoil and that a revolution was brewing.

'I've heard the same rumor,' Lawless

57

said. 'But without a leader, the people will resort to squabbling and nothin' will come of it.'

'This is what *El Presidente* is counting on. My people, they are like a snake without a head — ' He paused as an idea hit him, then exclaimed: '*Madre de Dios!*'

'What?'

'I have a thought. There is perhaps one *hombre* who might be able to help you find the señora — '

'Who?'

'Eloi Nunez.'

'Where do I find him?'

Ortega hesitated and chewed his lip uneasily.

'Well? Where is he?'

'Forgive me, my friend, but he is in jail.'

'So I'll bail him out.'

'Impossible. He is waiting to be executed.'

'Jesus. What'd he do?'

'Killed two *gringos*.'

'Then how the hell can he help me?'

Again Ortega hesitated and bit his lip.

'Dammit, spit it out.'

'My thought was . . . if you were to rescue him — ?'

'Rescue a murderer?'

'Nunez is not a murderer, *amigo*. These *gringos*, they rape his wife and daughter and deserved to die. But because they bribe Captain Aguilar, the evil that they did was ignored — '

'Aguilar?' Lawless repeated. 'Wait a minute. I know that name. Isn't he that no-good bastard who runs the local *rurales*?'

'*Si.*'

'So what you're sayin' is . . . the rural police have got Nunez locked up here, in Palomas?'

'That is sad but true.'

'When he's goin' to be executed?'

'Tomorrow morning. After the sun rises.'

Lawless silently groaned. 'Which means I break him out tonight or forget about it?'

Ortega hung his head. 'Forgive me, mi amigo. I am a fool to have mentioned his name.'

Mind churning, Lawless said: 'Before I stick my head in a noose, what makes you think this Nunez fella might know where Mrs. Albright is?'

Ortega looked around to make sure no one was listening before saying quietly: 'Because once, before he take a wife and have children, he was a bandido jefe, whose men terrorized the foothills of the western Sierra Madre.'

''Be damned,' Lawless said. 'An' you reckon if I bust him loose, and don't get shot for my trouble, Nunez will be so grateful he'll lead me to the bandits who kidnapped her?'

'This is my hope, yes.'

Lawless sighed and shook his head as if he couldn't believe he was even considering the idea.

'What're the names of his wife and young uns?' he asked finally.

Ortega frowned, wondering why Lawless needed to know, but said anyway: 'Teresa . . . Hector and Emilio.'

Lawless silently repeated the names to himself, then said: 'I'm goin' to need to think this over.'

'That is wise,' Ortega agreed. 'Meanwhile, let us finish our tequila and then enjoy supper. It is always best to make an important decision on a full stomach.'

8

It was dark when Lawless reined up at the corral beside the jail. A large, sprawling adobe building shaped like an L, it also served as headquarters for the local *rurales* under the command of Captain Armando Aguilar, a cruel, ruthless, corrupt man who was known to favor *gringos* over Mexicans. Not that he was prejudiced against his own people; he merely knew that *gringos* usually had more money, enabling them to offer him bigger bribes.

There were a dozen or so horses in the corral and they stirred restlessly as Lawless dismounted. His gray stallion nickered as Lawless tied it to the fence and swung around as if to kick him. Silently cursing it, he slapped the stallion on the rump with his hat, forcing it to step back. Lawless then jammed his hat back on his head and moved close to the wall of the sand-colored building.

Three barred cell-windows told him this side was the jail. Satisfied, Lawless looked toward the barracks that jutted out from the rear of the building. Lights showed in the windows and he could hear the men talking and laughing inside. Not seeing any sentries, he walked around to the front of the building.

Two *rurales* stood talking on the steps leading up to the entrance. They stared suspiciously at him, but said nothing. Lawless nodded politely to them and ducked in through the doorway.

Inside, a long hallway divided the jail from the officers' quarters. Halfway along it, Lawless stopped as a sergeant stepped out of an office marked CAPITAN A. AGUILAR. He looked upset, as if he'd just been chewed out, and was trying to light a cigarillo with trembling fingers.

Lawless flared a match on his jeans

and held the flame up to the cigarillo. The policeman inhaled deeply, blew out a lungful of smoke and nodded his thanks to Lawless before hurrying out.

Lawless knocked on the half-open door and entered.

A large, dark-haired man of fifty sat behind a desk, sopping up meat and beans with a rolled tortilla. His gray, silver-braided uniform was open at the throat and his red tie, sabre and large, high-crowned sombrero hung on a rack behind him. Once handsome and slim, his love of eating and drinking had given him a belly and bloated his face, while his rubbery dark eyes were almost hidden behind pouches of fat.

Those eyes were now focused on the tall, big-shouldered *gringo* facing him across his desk. '*Que quieres, señor?*'

'I'm here to see the prisoner,' Lawless said.

'That is impossible, señor. Not even his family can see him.'

'I was afraid of that,' Lawless said. 'Makes sense too. You let the wrong fella in, *commandante*, and next thing you know one of his friends has helped him escape.' He started to leave then paused and looked back, as if troubled. 'It's just that I owe Nunez money and wanted to pay him before he was executed.'

Captain Aguilar stopped in the middle of stuffing his face and suddenly looked interested. '*Dinero, señor?*'

'*Si*, two hundred dollars in gold eagles.' Lawless pulled a bulging leather pouch from his pocket and jiggled it so that the contents clinked. 'But, I reckon since Nunez will be feet-up in a few hours, it'd be a waste of time to give it to him now and have it end up in his grave.'

Captain Aguilar's dark eyes glittered with greed. '*Un momento, señor*,' he said as Lawless turned to go. 'Perhaps I was too hasty in turning you away.'

'No, you were right, *El Comman-dante* — '

'*Capitan*,' corrected Aguilar. 'Though I have long deserved to be promoted to *commandante* I have no important relatives to speak up for me, and promotions, they take forever in the *rurales*.'

'That seems unfair,' Lawless said. 'From what I've heard, you're a man of considerable stature and daring.' As Aguilar swelled pompously, Lawless added: 'As far as the money's concerned, I was just tryin' to do the honorable thing — '

'And so you shall, señor. Come.' The large, fleshy captain rose and took keys from his desk drawer. 'I'll take you to Nunez personally.'

'Well, if you're sure it ain't too much trouble . . . '

Captain Aguilar beamed. 'No trouble at all, señor. Come. Follow me.' He went to a thick, heavy door at the rear of the room, unlocked it and stood back so Lawless could enter.

'Here,' Lawless said, 'you better take my gun. Don't want the prisoner makin' a grab for it.' He handed his Colt to the captain and entered the jail.

Inside, moonlight shined in through the three barred windows. By its silvery light Lawless could see only the end cell was occupied. As he and Aguilar drew level with it, Lawless saw a shabbily dressed man of sixty or more lying on a pile of urine-smelling straw in the far corner.

'Stand up!' Captain Aguilar told him. 'You have a visitor.'

The man, who was short and wiry with a stubbly graying black beard, defiantly ignored the command and continued to lay there, arms folded behind his head.

'Get up, you worthless pig,' Aguilar hissed. 'Or I will have you beaten senseless.'

Worried that the man might not obey, Lawless said quickly: 'Señor Nunez, it's me, Lawless. I'm here to pay you your money.'

Curious, Eloi Nunez sat up and peered at the tall *Norteamericano* on the other side of the bars.

'Even if you don't need it for

yourself,' Lawless went on, 'surely you don't want Teresea or Hector an' Emilio to miss out on two hundred in gold?'

Nunez continued to stare at Lawless; finally, not recognizing him, he got to his feet and approached the bars.

'*Quien eres, señor?*'

'Name's Lawless. I'm from El Paso.'

'How is it you know the names of my wife and sons?'

Before Lawless could answer, Capitan Aguilar looked suspiciously at him, saying: 'If he is a friend of yours, *gringo*, how is it he doesn't recognize you?'

'I never said he was a friend,' Lawless replied. 'Truth is I've never seen him before — ' With that, he swung the bulging pouch as hard as he could against the side of the captain's head.

Aguilar collapsed without a sound . . . pebbles from the ripped pouch pouring all over him.

Lawless hunkered down and pulled his Colt from the captain's belt. Then unbuttoning the flap of the officer's holster, he grabbed the pistol and quickly handed it through the bars to Nunez.

'Here, take this.' Picking up the keys, he unlocked the door and grasping the captain by his boots, dragged him into the cell. 'Find something to gag him with,' he told the surprised Nunez, 'while I tie him up.'

Nunez untied his grimy neckerchief and gagged Aguilar with it. Meanwhile, Lawless used the captain's belt to bind his hands behind him, then ripped the filthy tattered blanket that lay on the straw in half and used one strip to tie up his ankles.

'*Vamonos!*' he told Nunez. '*Prisa!*'

They hurried from the cell. Lawless locked the captain inside while Nunez peered out the door leading to the captain's office. It was empty. He signaled to Lawless that all was clear and together they entered the room. Locking the jail door, Lawless threw the keys under the desk. He then grabbed a gray overcoat with silver epaulets that hung on a rack. 'Here, put this on.' He tossed it to Nunez.

It was much too large for the short and wiry former bandit, but it covered the loose-fitting white cotton rags he was wearing, reaching almost to his ankles; and when he slipped his bare feet into an extra pair of black boots that had just been polished, he resembled a Mexican caricature of Napoleon.

For a moment both men looked at each other in amusement, then they went out into the hallway. Two corporals stood smoking by the entrance. Lawless and Nunez waited until the policemen were looking the other way, then hurried to the rear entrance and ducked outside.

9

The two of them ran to the corral. Lawless took his lariat from his saddle, shook out a loop, twirled it and roped the nearest horse — a leggy sorrel with saddle burns on its back. Meanwhile Nunez opened the gate, entered the corral and ran to the roped horse. Already broken, it didn't offer much resistance and Nunez grabbed the mane and vaulted onto its back.

Lawless untied the stallion, swung up onto his own saddle and waited for Nunez to ride out of the corral. 'Leave it open,' he yelled as Nunez went to close the gate. 'Without horses, they can't follow us.' He fired two shots in the air and the panicked horses burst out of the corral and ran off into the night.

Instantly, lights went on in the barracks. Men began shouting to one another and within moments some of them, half-dressed, came pouring out. Lawless fired several shots above their heads, making them hit the dirt, then he and Nunez kicked their horses into a gallop and rode off.

They didn't stop until they were out of town and had taken cover behind a rocky outcrop. There, Nunez demanded to know who Lawless really was and why he'd broken him out of jail.

Lawless quickly explained.

Before he was finished, Nunez interrupted him and said: '*Perdoname, por favor, señor* — you say you are a friend of Angel Ortega's?'

Lawless nodded. 'We've been pals for years.'

'And this is why you save me from a firing squad? — so I can help you find Señora Albright?'

'Yeah — and her husband. I figure it's the least you can do in return for me savin' your neck.'

Nunez studied Lawless for a moment, then smiled. 'It is indeed. But first, señor, we must ride to the *sierras*. Once there, I promise you the *rurales* will never find us.'

'Sounds good to me,' Lawless said. 'Lead the way.'

They rode all night, occasionally spelling the horses, and by dawn could see the massive peaks of the Sierra Madre Occidental in the far distance. Dismounting beside a rock formation that overlooked a dry riverbed, they allowed themselves and the horses a few precious drops of water from the extra canteen that Ortega had given Lawless, and then took a nap under a clump of ocotillo bushes.

They slept, undisturbed for several hours, then were awakened by a shrill whinny. Instantly Lawless sat up, at the same time reaching for his six-gun.

In front of him the hobbled stallion reared up in panic then came down with both hooves, attempting to stamp on something coiled in the sand before it.

Lawless saw the rattler draw its blunt

head back, ready to strike, and at the same time heard its whirring rattle. Barely aiming, he snapped off a shot and saw the snake's head explode, blood spattering over the stallion's pale gray forelegs.

Nearby, Nunez grabbed his pistol and jumped to his feet, ready to shoot any other rattlesnakes that might be around. There were none. He tucked the pistol in his belt and approached the jittery stallion, his voice soothing as he tried to calm it.

'Get back,' Lawless warned. 'The sonofabitch'll stomp you.'

Nunez ignored him and continued to speak softly in Spanish to the wild-eyed purebred.

Lawless watched in disbelief as the wiry little Mexican got close to the stallion, the horse snorting through its inflated, foam-flecked nostrils as it stood there quivering with fear.

'I'm warnin' you,' Lawless said. 'Touch him and he'll bite the hell out of you.'

Again Nunez ignored him. 'Easy . . . easy . . .' he whispered to the stallion. 'You do not want to bite me, do you, my handsome friend . . . Noooooo . . . You and I, we are as one . . . the same Spanish blood runs through our veins.' Slowly raising his hand, Nunez gently stroked the horse's proudly arched neck. 'There . . . there . . . relax. Calm yourself. I, Eloi Nunez, will not let anything harm you. This I promise.'

Gradually the pale gray stallion calmed down and nickered softly.

'He is fine now,' Nunez said to Lawless. 'He was just nervous.'

'When isn't he?' Lawless grumbled. 'Judas, he gets scared if a damn butterfly goes near him.'

'You misjudge him, *amigo*. What you see is not fear. A stallion of his quality . . . his ancestry . . . he knows no fear. These displays, they are his survival instincts.' He continued to stroke the stallion's neck and withers. Eventually the horse stopped quivering and made soft snuffling noises.

'I'll be goddamned,' said Lawless. 'If I hadn't seen it with my own eyes I never would've believed it. Hell, I would've bet my life that he'd bite you. Reckon you must have some kind of magical power over horses.'

Nunez smiled. 'No. No magic. No special power. They know I respect and honor them. They are God's most beautiful creatures. To watch a horse run, with its mane and tail flying in the wind, is as close to perfection as man will ever see.'

'If you say so,' Lawless grunted. He eyed the stallion as if it had betrayed him. 'Frankly, I ain't that fond of the brutes. Most horses I've ridden were mean as broomtails an' would just as soon stomp you or bite you than eat their oats.'

Nunez didn't respond but the look in his dark eyes clearly showed that he disagreed with Lawless. 'Well,' he said, 'at least *we* will eat well tonight.' Using his pistol he scooped up the dead rattler and held it up to Lawless. 'If you have a knife, señor, I will skin this for the pot. It will make good eating.'

Lawless pulled a folding knife from his jeans and tossed it to Nunez, saying: 'I'll build a fire.'

10

After their meal and a restful smoke, they again rode all night and by sunup had reached the foothills of the mighty western Sierra Madre. As they made their way through the deep sheer-walled canyons, climbing ever upward, Lawless asked Nunez why he thought the *bandidos* were holed up here.

'Because they know they are safe,' the former bandit replied. 'Not even the *rurales* dare enter these mountains.'

'Maybe the *rurales* won't attack them,' Lawless said, 'but what about Indians?'

Nunez smiled. 'The Tarahumara are a shy people. A long time ago they retreated into the sierras to avoid the Spanish explorers. They want no trouble. In all the time that I and my men rode here, we rarely caught a glimpse of them.'

'I've heard they can run down a deer?'

'It is true. That is how they hunt game — by using their great endurance to exhaust the animal and then killing it when it cannot resist. That is why they are known as 'The Runners.''

They rode for another mile or so in silence, the trail steepening and climbing through dense forests and around small, clear mountain lakes. Finally Lawless broke the silence by asking the question that had been chewing at him ever since he'd rescued Nunez. 'Tell me somethin', *hombre*: how come you speak American so well?'

'Jesuits,' Nunez replied. 'I was raised by them.'

Lawless almost laughed.

'You find this amusing, señor?'

'Lawless. Call me Lawless,' Lawless said, adding: 'Yeah, sort of. I mean, if you were taught to obey the Good Book, how'd you end up becomin' a bandit? Robbing and killin' folks ain't exactly one of the Ten Commandments.'

'Neither is kidnapping.'

'You were kidnapped?'

'*Si*. From the Jesuits — me and many other *niños*.'

'Who by?'

'*Bandidos*.'

'Why? What'd they want with young-uns?'

'They trained us to be' — he searched for the word — '*espias*.'

'Spies?'

'*Si*. Then when we grew older and were more experienced, they made us become bandits.'

'Uh-*huh*.' Lawless thought a moment before saying: 'From what Angel and his wife told me, you took to it real well.'

'This is true. But it is also true that I had the best of teachers, Heraclio Bernal.'

Lawless looked impressed. 'You rode with the Thunder Bolt of Sinaloa?'

'Till his death, *si*.'

80

'Why'd you quit?'

'After Bernal was ambushed by two of his own men, the Parra brothers took over. From then on there was much senseless killing.'

'I know. When I rode for Governor Vargas, he was always ranting about you.' Lawless chuckled. 'Told me once he'd gladly pay a million pesos to nail your hides.'

Nunez sighed, troubled by his memories. 'All this killing did not please me. Nor was I alone in my thinking. Many *hombres* were sickened by the slaughter. They, like me, remembered how it once was when we used to raid the silver mines in the Sierra Madre Occidental. Then, very few miners or their families were killed. But once Ignacio Parra became *jefe*, our orders were to shoot everyone, even those who did not resist us.'

'Is that when you quit?'

'*Si, señor.*'

'Lawless.'

Nunez thought of his past life and

then said: 'I did not plan my escape. Fate decided for me. It was during a raid in Barranca del Cobre. I was shot from my horse. I was only wounded, but as I lay there I realized this was my chance to stop riding for the Parras without having them shoot me. So I faked my death. And after everyone had ridden off, I crawled away and hid in a cave until my wound healed. Then I made my way to Palomas, where I changed my name to Nunez and began a new life.'

'And now,' Lawless said, 'I reckon you'll have to change your name again and begin another life someplace else — 'less you plan on facin' a firing squad.'

Nunez shrugged, resigned. '*Que es vida.*'

They rode on, through deep craggy ravines and past lakes mirroring the blue sky, the rocky terrain often so steep they had to dismount and walk their horses.

By midday they were above the

foothills and by craning their necks could see the peaks of the towering mountains. Here, beside a shallow creek half-hidden by rocks, Nunez stopped his horse and told Lawless to wait there for him.

'Why? Where you goin'?'

'To ask about the señora's where-abouts.'

'Ask who?' Lawless said, looking about them. 'I don't see anyone.'

Nunez smiled as if he knew a secret. '*Sea paciente, mi amigo.*' He kneed his horse forward and rode on along the steep, winding mountain trail.

Again Lawless scanned the rocky cliffs surrounding them, but saw no one.

'How long they been watchin' us?' he called out.

Nunez's voice floated back to him. '*Pregunte a su cabello. El sabra.*' The former bandit disappeared around a bend ahead.

Lawless dismounted, tied the reins around a dead tree stump, loosened the cinch strap and pulled his rifle from its scabbard.

'Like hell I will,' he told the stallion. 'Day I ask you anythin' will be the day I plug you 'tween the eyes.'

The stallion pricked its ears and bared its big yellow teeth at Lawless and nickered as if laughing at him.

11

Nunez did not return.

Lawless made himself comfortable in the shade of an overhanging rock, and smoked away the hours. But as the cigarette butts piled up beside him and there was still no sign of Nunez, he wondered if the former bandit had ducked out on him or, worse, run into trouble.

The stallion knew better. It suddenly pricked its ears, hearing what Lawless couldn't, and snorted nervously.

'What?' Lawless said, reaching for his rifle. 'D'you hear somethin'? Is someone comin'?'

Moments later he heard the sound of horses approaching, their hooves clattering on the scattered rocks about the trail. Rising, he hid behind a rock and waited to see who it was. Shortly three riders appeared around the bend in the trail ahead. Judging by their grubby appearance, high-crowned sombreros and twin *bandoleros* crossed over their chests, he guessed they were *bandidos*.

Stepping out from behind the rock, he leveled his Winchester at them. 'That's close enough!'

The leader, a slim, dark-haired, fierce-eyed young boy — no, woman, he realized — reined up and motioned for her companions to do the same.

'Lower your rifle, Señor Lawless,' she said. 'We are not here to harm you.'

Keeping the rifle trained on them, Lawless said: 'Where's Señor Nunez?'

'In camp, talking to El Flaco about a *gringo* woman.'

Lawless saw only defiance and honesty in her dark eyes and decided she was telling the truth.

'Where is this camp?'

'In the *Cañon de Muchas Cuevas*,' she replied, adding: 'It is not far.'

Again he sensed she was telling the truth. Lowering his Winchester, he walked to his horse. Slipping the rifle into its scabbard, he tightened the saddle cinch and mounted the stallion.

But as he rode on along the winding trail, with the young woman beside him and the two men bringing up the rear, Lawless kept his hand on his six-gun just in case he was being led into a trap.

'*Como te llamas?*' he asked her as they left the trail and entered a narrow canyon with sheer white walls riddled with caves.

'What is my name to you?' she replied, her tone as fiery as her look.

'Nothin'. Just wondered.'

'It is your plan to tell the *rurales* about me?'

'Plan? I don't have a plan. An' even if I did it wouldn't include me turnin' you in to Capitan Aguilar. He's no friend of mine. Neither are the *rurales*.' Then as she continued to glare suspiciously at him: 'I reckon Señor Nunez didn't tell you that I'm the one who busted him out of their jail?'

'He did not tell *me* anything,' she snapped. 'Why would he? I do not give orders, I take them.'

'Well, I did,' Lawless said. 'An' I hog-tied the *commandante* and locked him in one of the cells!'

The young woman frowned, puzzled. 'Why do you tell me this?'

'So you don't think I'll turn you in to the *rurales*.'

'I would shoot you if you tried, *gringo*. Remember that.'

'I will,' Lawless said. 'But I'd still like to know your name.'

She shrugged. 'Mateos.'

'I meant your first name.'

'Catarina.'

'*Muy bonito.*'

She looked insulted. 'I am no flower to be pampered by rich men. I can ride and shoot as well as any man.'

Lawless chuckled. 'I don't doubt it. Look,' he added when she scowled, 'I meant that as a compliment, not an insult.'

The bandits behind them laughed, their taunting adding to Catarina's anger.

'*Hombres!*' she hissed. 'You will never know the true worth of a woman.' Digging her spurs in, she rode on ahead, soon lost among the rocks and trees.

'Mite touchy, ain't she?' Lawless said to one of the bandits.

The man grunted and spat his disgust into the dirt. 'Catarina, she does not tease well,' he growled.

'She does not cook well either,' said the other bandit. 'Unlucky the man who marries her.'

There's more to life than cooking, Lawless thought. Then trying to visualize it: *One thing's for true, it'd be no hardship wakin' up beside her every mornin'.*

High above them a hawk drifted on the thermals, shrieking. Lawless gazed up at it and for the first time noticed a lookout with a rifle standing on the rim of the canyon. Lawless looked at the opposite rim and saw another armed lookout. This one, on spotting them, removed his sombrero and waved it twice over his head, signaling to someone behind and below him that Lawless couldn't see.

'Friends of yours?' Lawless asked the uglier of the two bandits.

'They are warning the camp that we are coming,' the man replied. 'This way, they do not shoot us.'

'I'm all for that,' Lawless said.

They rode through a stand of pine-oaks and came out into a wide mountain meadow that was bright with wild flowers. Ahead, the Canyon of Many Caves narrowed even more and then seemed to dead-end at a wall of sheer rock. But as they got close Lawless saw several more caves among the rocks. Most of them were too small to live in or even hide in but one was just wide enough to ride through. They approached it and led by the ugly bandit, ducked their heads and guided their horses between the rocks, both sides close enough for Lawless to feel the rock scraping against his knees.

Shortly, they reached the other end

and rode out into a natural open hollow that Lawless guessed had been formed millions of years ago by a lake. A shallow stream ran through it, fed by a thin waterfall that cascaded down from an opening in the surrounding cliffs. Laughing children played in the sparkling water and brightly-clad women washed and pummeled their laundry on the flat rocks along the water's edge.

'Some set-up you got here,' Lawless said as they rode toward the largest of the caves. 'No wonder the *rurales* couldn't find you.'

'We would welcome them if they did,' the ugly bandit said and winked at his companion, who laughed and for Lawless's benefit drew his finger across his throat.

They reined up and dismounted in front of the large cave. Three bandits emerged, all heavily armed, their sour expressions warning Lawless that he wasn't welcome.

One man, whose strutting walk and sneering demeanor exuded authority, confronted Lawless and demanded he hand over his gun. When Lawless started to refuse, the other two bandits instantly aimed their rifles at him.

'Do you wish to die, *gringo?*' The man stuck out his hand as he spoke and Lawless grudgingly handed over his rifle and six-gun. 'I am Lucero Dominguez,' he added haughtily. 'You have heard of me?'

'Uh-uh.'

Lucero looked pityingly at him. 'You will, señor. One day your children will read books about me in school.'

'Can't wait to start a family,' Lawless said.

Lucero ignored his sarcasm, turned and motioned for Lawless to follow him. Lawless obeyed. The other bandits, rifles aimed at his back, followed.

12

Inside, the shadowy high-ceilinged cave was big enough to accommodate fifty men. At the rear several women worked around an open fire. Some were stirring kettles of chicken and beans while others crouched over flat stones, grinding corn or rolling out tortillas, their giant shadows flickering on the walls.

Most of the smoke spiraled upward, escaping through cracks in the ceiling. What smoke remained hung in the air like a shroud, making Lawless's eyes water.

Lucero led him to a group of men gathered against one wall. They were swarthy, hard-eyed men with sombreros pushed back off their heads, pistols stuck in their pants, machetes hanging from their belts and rifles resting across their knees. They sat in a circle, talking in low tones, their voices respectful whenever they addressed their leader, El Flaco.

Tall and gaunt with long black hair and black, unforgiving eyes El Flaco was dressed no differently than his men. Nor were there any silver conchos adorning his nearby saddle or on the black leather band around his crown of his sombrero. Yet there was something about him, Lawless realized as he stopped in front of the bandit leader, that set him apart — a charismatic presence that seemed to radiate from him even when he wasn't talking or gesturing.

Seated beside El Flaco was Eloi Nunez, and as soon as he saw Lawless approaching he got up, smiling and extending his hand.

'Forgive me for not returning,' he said quietly, so only Lawless could hear. 'But it was more important that I stay here and persuade El Flaco not to kill you.'

'Glad you did,' Lawless said, shaking hands. 'I got a feelin' I don't have many friends around here.' He gazed about him as he spoke, looking for Tess Albright and her husband.

'They are safe,' Nunez said, reading his mind. 'But I fear you will not be pleased when you learn the truth.'

'Sit down, *gringo*,' El Flaco ordered before Lawless could answer. He motioned to one of the bandits seated opposite him, and the man grudgingly rose and moved away. 'There, where I can read your eyes while we talk.'

Lawless obeyed, while Nunez returned to his place beside the bandit leader.

'My English, it not so good,' El Flaco said, adding: '*Hablas español?*'

Lawless nodded. '*Un poquito.*'

'I will translate for you if you like?' Nunez offered.

'Thanks. If I get in over my head, I'll ask you to do that.' To El Flaco, he added in Spanish: 'I'm looking for a woman, Mrs. Albright, and her husband. They were kidnapped just across the border a few days ago. Have you seen them?'

The bandit leader glanced questioningly at Nunez before answering Lawless. 'They are here, *gringo*. But you are mistaken. They were not kidnapped. They came here of their own free will.'

Lawless stared into El Flaco's unflinching, deep-set black eyes and though he didn't understand why, sensed he was telling the truth.

'If they're here, then I'd like to talk to them.'

'I would allow this, but they said they did not want to talk to you.'

Lawless looked at Nunez. 'Maybe I misunderstood him,' he said in English, 'but did he just say the Albrights didn't want to talk to me?'

Then as Nunez nodded:

'That's *loco*. Mrs. Albright's the one who hired me back in New Mexico — paid me to come down here and find her husband, Tucker.'

'I know that. But I spoke to her myself, *mi amigo* — she *and* her husband — and that's what she told me.' Pausing, he then said something in

Spanish to El Flaco. The bandit leader looked surprised. He started to shake his head, then changed his mind and whispered in Nunez's ear. Nunez nodded and said something that made El Flaco frown and think for a moment, as if making a decision. Then he turned to Lawless and in Spanish said:

'I have decided to let you speak to the woman.'

'*Bueno.*' Lawless got to his feet.

'Go with him,' El Flaco told Nunez. 'If any of my men try to kill him, warn them that Señor Lawless is under my protection.'

13

Nunez led Lawless from the cave to another, much smaller, more secluded cave behind some trees. On their way they passed a group of displaced *campesinos* and their families, all gathered in a makeshift camp like refugees. Dressed in their traditional white cotton, the men stopped what they were doing to glare at Lawless and make threatening gestures as he walked past.

'Is it just me or do they hate all *gringos?*' Lawless asked Nunez.

'All. It is sad but understandable,' he added. 'These people have been driven out of their *pueblos* and farms from here to Juarez. Their whole lives they lived in fear of renegades, *gringos* who burned their homes, raped and stole their women then rode back across the border. Now, here, thanks to El Flaco, they feel safe and — '

'Seein' me reopens those old wounds, right?'

Nunez nodded. 'One day, hopefully, things will change, and we and our *Norteamericano* neighbors will be able to live in peace together.'

'It's a pretty thought,' Lawless said grimly. 'But I wouldn't hang my hat on it.'

They reached the entrance to the cave, stopped, and Nunez called out to the Albrights.

Within moments a tall, big-shouldered, sandy-haired man in his late thirties appeared. He was handsome in a weak, sullen way and wore expensive black, silver-trimmed clothes and hand-tooled boots like a *rico hacendado*. But he didn't act like a rich rancher; he acted like a spoiled petulant boy used to getting his way.

'*Que quiere?*' he demanded.

'I want to talk to your wife,' Lawless said.

'What about?'

'That's 'tween me an' her.'

'Then it'll have to keep. Tess doesn't want to talk to anyone.'

'She'll talk to me.'

'Why? Who the devil are you?'

'Name's Lawless. She hired me to — '

'No, no, you're the last person she wants to see. Now take a hike!'

'Not until I talk to Mrs. Albright,' Lawless said stubbornly. 'Better get her, mister — or I'll have to come in there and get her myself.'

Tucker Albright started to bluster; then something in Lawless's narrowed pale gray eyes warned him not to argue with this man.

'Wait here,' he said. Turning, he disappeared into the cave.

'Friendly sort, ain't he?' Lawless said, rolling his eyes at Nunez. 'Wonder what the hell his wife ever saw in him?'

Nunez said only: 'Do not get your hopes up, *mi amigo*. As I told you earlier, this is not how it seems.'

Before Lawless could ask him what

100

he meant, Tess Albright appeared in the mouth of the cave. Her normally neat riding clothes were rumpled, her tawny curls a tangled mess, and she looked bruised and defeated.

Lawless could scarcely believe it was the same audaciously defiant young woman he'd met in the lawyer's office in Deming.

'Ma'am,' he said, politely removing his hat. 'Good to see you again.'

Tess tried to smile, failed, lowered her eyes and said brusquely: 'You shouldn't have come, Mr. Lawless.'

'Didn't have much choice.'

'If this is about your money,' she said, glancing behind her as if expecting trouble, 'I'm not trying to cheat you. Mr. Herd, the lawyer you met in Deming, has already given the bank instructions to pay you what I owe you.'

'This ain't about money,' Lawless said, stung. 'I came here to get you and your husband, and take you both back home.'

Tess hesitated. Lawless saw uneasiness

101

in her sad blue eyes, and wasn't surprised when she said: 'I . . . uh . . . made a mistake.'

'Ma'am?'

'I was wrong. Tuck wasn't kidnapped, like I thought. He was in Palomas on business. He and Señor Suarez are — '

'Suarez?'

Nunez nudged him. 'That's El Flaco's real name — Eduardo Suarez.'

'What kind of business?' Lawless asked, turning back to Tess, ' — robbing trains an' stagecoaches an' silver mines?'

Before she could reply Tucker reappeared and forcefully put his arm around her, saying: 'My business with Señor Suarez is none of your concern, Lawless.'

'No. But gettin' your wife home safely is.'

'Don't worry about Tess,' Tucker said belligerently. 'She's my wife, and I'll damn well take care of her any way I see fit.'

Lawless ignored Tucker and turned to Tess. ''fore I go, ma'am, answer me one question — are you here 'cause you want to be or because your husband's forcin' you to stay?'

Tess hesitated, tight-lipped, before saying: 'Because I want to be, of course. If I didn't, I'd leave.'

Lawless didn't believe her. He saw a glimmer of hope in her blue eyes, but only for an instant. Then it was gone. And she once more looked defeated — an emotion that he never would have believed existed in her when they first met.

'Okay, you got your answer,' Tucker told Lawless. 'And like Tess said, your money's at the bank in Deming. So get on your damn horse, mister, and ride out of here. Leave us the hell alone. C'mon, honey,' he added, 'you got nothing more to say to this man.' Arm still around her, he muscled her back into the cave.

Lawless looked questioningly at Nunez, who shrugged and said: 'You have done all you can, *mi amigo*. To try to do more or stay here beyond tonight will only result in your death.'

'For chrissake,' Lawless said, flaring, 'can't you see what's goin' on? The bastard's got her buffaloed.'

'That is not our business, as Señor Albright so clearly pointed out.'

'Yeah? Well, I intend to *make* it my business,' Lawless said grimly.

'*Por que?*'

''cause I don't cotton to women bein' held prisoner — 'specially a woman who hired me to help her.'

'Why would Señor Albright hold his wife prisoner?'

'I don't know — yet. All I know is she lied to me just now an' I don't peg her as the lyin' kind.'

'What did the señora lie about?'

'Said her lawyer in Deming had already told the bank to pay me the money she owes me. And that's impossible.'

'Forgive me, but why?'

''cause there's no telegraph around here.'

Nunez frowned, puzzled. 'I do not follow you.'

'It's simple. Mrs. Albright couldn't have known I was comin' down here.'

'Why not? You said she already paid you half of your money.'

'To find her husband, yeah. Not her. Hell, she wasn't even kidnapped back then.' Lawless paused, then said: 'And just for argument's sake, even if she had somehow found out I was comin', she still would've needed the telegraph to notify the bank. What's more,' he added, 'when her husband came out, he repeated what she said almost word for word — which most likely means he told her what to say while they were still back in the cave together.'

There was logic in that, Nunez had to admit.

'An' before you call me *loco*,' Lawless went on, 'chew on this: accordin' to Mrs. Albright, before her husband was supposedly kidnapped, he'd been making regular trips to Palomas. When she called him on it, know what he told her? — that it was because he found the local women 'entertaining.''

Nunez looked incredulous. 'He actually told her this?'

'Yeah.' Lawless shook his head. 'I couldn't believe it either. That's when I started thinking that somethin' mighty odd was goin' on. I mean what husband in his right mind would willingly admit to his wife that he's enjoyin' other women — 'specially a woman who holds the purse strings?'

'None that I know of,' agreed Nunez.

'Me neither. It was then I realized he must've done it deliberately, hopin' to keep her mind off the real reason.'

'Which is what?' asked Nunez.

'Beats me. But I bet it's tied in with her bein' snatched an' brought down here. I mean, if she disappeared in New Mexico, he'd have the law breathin' down his neck. But here, who's goin' to question it or blame him? Certainly no law north of the border. They'd just figure it was another kidnappin' by *bandidos* and make an official protest to the Mexican government, then go on about their business.'

Nunez mulled things over before saying: 'I have heard it said that the Albrights possess much land and money. Is this true?'

'Yep. She inherited it from her folks. Then there's another odd thing. Accordin' to their lawyer, the husband was in Mexico tryin' to buy up more land south of the border.'

Nunez made a scoffing sound. 'The *rancheros*, they would never sell their land to a *gringo*.'

'Exactly. So obviously the sonofabitch was involved in somethin' else — but what, I've no idea.' Lawless paused as angry voices quarreling could be heard inside the cave. There was a sudden loud slap followed by a cry of pain from Tess.

'No! Wait.' Nunez grabbed Lawless's arm, stopping him from entering the cave.

'Let go,' Lawless said. Then as Nunez still held him: 'I ain't askin' you to get involved, but I'm not standin' by while that weak-livered bastard beats on her.'

Nunez looked up at Lawless, a fire building in his dark eyes. 'I would not ask you to — or expect you to.'

'Then let go.'

'First, listen to me. If you want to help the señora, then you must be patient. To try to take her out of here now will only buy you a bullet — and perhaps her too. But if you wait until later, when it is dark, you'll not only have a better chance of saving her, but I will help you.'

Lawless shook his head. 'Hell, I can't ask you to do that.'

'You are not asking me, *mi amigo*. I am offering.'

'You do know the chances of pullin' this off are slim an' none, don't you?'

Nunez smiled — a weary, wistful smile reeking of sadness. 'My wife, may God bless her, has passed on, my children are grown and I see my grandchildren so seldom they cannot remember who I am. This is no way to live.'

Lawless couldn't argue with that. 'There's somethin' else you ought to consider: could be I'm wrong about Mrs. Albright. Could be she really did come down here because she wanted to. If that's the case — '

Nunez cut him off. 'Either way, it would warm this old *pistolero's* heart if I could die as a man should die — fighting to help others less fortunate. Besides,' he added with a wry smile. 'I know where their horses are hidden. If we stampede them out of the canyon, it will give us a head start before they can round them up and follow us.'

Lawless had to admit that it made sense. Grateful, he offered Nunez his hand. '*Amigo*,' he said, 'you just dealt yourself in on this fight.'

14

The cliffs and hillsides were full of caves. Lawless and Nunez chose one that could only be reached by climbing up a short rocky slope. Facing the cave was a small, dense wood. Leaving their hobbled horses to feed on the grass growing in front of the trees, they climbed up the rocks and entered the cave. Inside, there was enough room for about four people, but the arched roof was high enough so that even Lawless, tall as he was, could stand up. Everything smelled faintly of stale smoke.

They moved to the rear of the cave and spread their blankets on the ground beside a pile of dead ashes that remained from a previous fire.

'Reckon we'll eat cold tonight,' Lawless said as they sat with their backs against the wall. 'Don't need to give anyone out there a target to shoot at.'

Nunez nodded and gently rubbed the aches from his body. 'This growing old,' he said, wincing, 'it is not for the faint-hearted.'

'What is in life?' Lawless replied. He took two hardtack biscuits from his saddlebag and handed one to Nunez. 'Just tryin' to get through every day, dusk till dawn, wears a fella clean out.' He munched on the hard biscuit, adding: 'Sure wish I had some coffee to dunk this in.'

Nunez grunted. 'So do my teeth — what few I have remaining.' He broke the hardtack into small pieces, put one in his mouth, waited until his saliva softened it a little and then gingerly bit down. '*Bueno*,' he said, adding: 'El Flaco's father, who rode with me, he once became ill from something and lost all his teeth. He carved himself some wooden ones, but they hurt so badly when he bit down that eventually he sold them to an old *gitana* — ' He paused as he saw that

Lawless didn't understand, then said: 'One you call a fortune-teller.'

'Ahh. Like a gypsy?'

'*Si*. A *Hungaro*. She lived alone in the foothills in Sinaloa. I knew her well and often after a raid I would give her food. She had no money but insisted on repaying me by telling me my fortune.' He grunted, amused by his thoughts, then said: 'I do not believe in this fortune-telling and I told Hajna that.'

'What'd she say?'

'She laughed as if she knew a dark secret. Then she grabbed my hand, stared at my palm for several moments and then quickly looked away. When I asked her what she saw, she dropped my hand and hurried off. One of my men, Rafael, said he'd only seen her look that way once before, when she saw death in the hand of one of his cousins.'

'No magic there,' Lawless said. 'Hell, we're all goin' to die. Just how that matters.'

'*Valientemente*.'

'Yeah,' said Lawless. 'That's how I'd like to go out, too.'

There was a faint noise outside. Both looked at the entrance, Lawless quickly drawing his gun, saying: ''less you want to get shot, show yourself.'

Almost immediately a slim figure appeared in the mouth of the cave. 'It's me — Tess,' she said. She came closer and though the light was poor and her once-pretty face was now bruised and swollen, Lawless recognized Mrs. Albright.

Rising, he put his arm about her, steadying her, and led her to his blanket. 'Sit here,' he said. He gently lowered her to the blanket and then sat beside her.

'Who did this — your husband?'

She looked down, embarrassed to meet his gaze. 'H-He . . . it's not all his fault,' she said, her words slurred by her swollen split lips. 'He has a terrible temper and I . . . have not gone out of my way to please him lately.'

'That's no excuse,' Lawless said. 'He's

still a man an' men ain't supposed to beat on women — not for any reason. And I aim to bounce that off his memory next time I run into him.'

As if not listening, Tess said: 'Tuck thinks I've betrayed him.'

'Then he's a fool,' Lawless said. 'I don't believe you'd do that no more than I believe you'd lie without bein' forced to.'

She didn't reply, but her blue eyes thanked him.

'But even if you had — did,' he continued, 'he's a fine one to talk after tellin' you he keeps company in Palomas.'

'No, no, you misunderstand,' Tess said. 'Not because I slept with another man — I doubt if that would even bother Tuck right now. He means about . . . ' She caught herself and didn't finish.

''bout what?' Lawless pressed. When she didn't answer, he added: 'What you say here stays here. You can count on that.'

Tess suddenly buried her face in her hands and wept.

Lawless, like most strong, rugged men, had no answer for tears. He looked at Nunez, asking for help, but the ageing former bandit had no answer either.

'Don't . . . please don't,' Lawless said uncomfortably. 'I can't handle tears.'

'I'm s-sorry.' She sniffed back her tears, adding: 'I hate weepy women, too. But lately — well, I'm ashamed to say, I seem to be crying a lot.'

'Señora . . . ' Nunez leaned forward and gave Tess his kerchief so she could wipe her eyes. '*Por favor* . . . this betrayal you speak of . . . perhaps if you tell what it is, we can help you.'

'We'd sure try,' put in Lawless.

Tess sighed wearily. 'Tuck thinks . . . I . . . told the authorities about . . . Oh, dear God.' Again she covered her face with her hands but this time, she didn't cry.

''Bout what?' Lawless demanded.

'*La revolucion*,' she blurted.

Lawless and Nunez swapped puzzled looks.

'What revolution?'

'The one they're planning — he and Suarez and . . . others.'

Again Lawless and Nunez exchanged looks, but this time of surprise.

'Let me get this straight,' Lawless said to Tess. 'Your husband and El Flaco are plannin' on starting a revolution?'

'Yes.'

'Against who, Governor Vargas?'

'N-No — President Diaz.'

'The Mexican government?'

Lawless and Nunez looked even more surprised.

'Are they *loco*?'

'Señora,' Nunez said quietly, '*por favor*, this you know for true?'

Tess nodded slowly, as if she couldn't believe it herself.

Lawless said: 'This is the secret your husband lied about — the real reason why he kept goin' to Palomas?'

Again she nodded.

116

'When'd you find out about it?'

'Just before I was kidnapped. Tuck suddenly showed up at the ranch. Of course I was surprised and — and relieved, very relieved, but angry too and I kept asking him about his philandering and why he couldn't stay faithful to me. He told me to mind my own business, to shut up or else he'd leave me again and this time for good. But I couldn't. I didn't care by then. I kept after him, kept hounding him about it until suddenly he exploded, lost his temper completely and slapped me, kept slapping me until he knocked me down, all the time saying that women had nothing to do with it — that what he was involved in was far more important than women — any woman — even me. That's when I lost my temper as well, and said if he didn't tell me what was going on then he didn't have to worry about leaving me, 'cause I was leaving him — wanted him out of my house, right away, and was going to file for divorce.'

'What'd he say to that?' Lawless asked.

'He was — well, shocked, I guess you'd say. He knows I've always loved him so devotedly it felt as if he'd cast a spell over me. Hearing me actually say I'd leave was something he never expected.'

'How'd he react?'

'He calmed down a little and asked me if I was serious, really intended to get a divorce. When I said yes, unless he told me the truth, he thought about it for a moment, then shrugged and said there weren't any other women — in Palomas or anywhere else. He said it quietly, you know, without any of his usual blustering, and when I looked in his eyes I could tell he was telling me the truth. So I said if he wasn't involved with other women, what *was* he involved in? That's when he said: 'If I tell you, Tess, you can't tell anyone. If you do, men will come here and kill you, men much more powerful than me, and no matter what I do or say, I won't be able to stop them. Do you understand that?' I said I did, and that no matter what it was I would keep it a secret.'

'An' that's when he told you about startin' a rebellion against President Diaz?' Lawless said.

Tess nodded. 'At first I didn't believe him. I mean, Tuck has never been interested in politics of any kind — or Mexico itself for that matter — except for trying to buy the ranches bordering ours. He's always wanted those. In fact I'm sure that's what's behind it,' she went on — 'the chance to own all the ranches on the other side of the border — ranches that he'll never be able to buy so long as the present government is in office.'

Nunez sighed painfully before asking: 'So this is how El Flaco bought your husband's loyalty — by offering him the *rancheros?*'

'I think so, yes.'

'There's got to be someone else

behind it, someone much more powerful,' Lawless said to Nunez. 'El Flaco — hell, he may run roughshod over the farmers and miners in these mountains but to me he's change. Saphead like him, he don't have the money or the clout to overthrow Porfirio Diaz's government.'

'True,' Nunez said. 'But there is one man who does.'

'Vargas!' Lawless exclaimed as it hit him.

'*Si*. For years now it has been well-known that his greed and lust for power could never be satisfied by just being governor of Chihuahua.'

Lawless grunted. 'Figures,' he said wryly. 'I come down here knowin' I'm stickin' my head in a noose. But I ain't content with that. No, sir. I got to step right into a hornets' nest as well.'

'I'm sorry,' Tess said quietly. 'When I asked you to find Tuck for me, I had no idea what was really going on.'

'Hell, I know that,' Lawless said good-naturedly. 'It's just the nature of things. Trouble follows me around like a lost shadow.'

Nunez thought of something and chuckled. '*El agitador.*'

'That's me all right,' admitted Lawless. 'Just ask anyone wearin' a star.'

Tess, who'd been studying him, now said gently: 'I don't believe you're a troublemaker. I'm starting to think you're a pretty decent man.'

It was said so sincerely, with so much warmth that Lawless was stumped for a comeback.

'I'm sorry,' Tess said, 'I didn't mean to embarrass you.'

Lawless started to tell her he wasn't embarrassed — then stopped as he heard someone climbing up the rocks to the cave. Motioning for the others to be quiet, he reached for his rifle and levered in a round.

Moments later, a shadowy figure appeared in the mouth of the cave.

Lawless raised his rifle, ready to shoot, but Nunez quickly knocked his arm down.

'*Buenas tardes, mi abuelo,*' the intruder said politely.

Lawless, on recognizing the young woman, turned to Nunez in surprise. 'This is — she's your granddaughter?'

'*Si,*' Nunez smiled and embraced the young woman. 'It has been a long time, Catarina.'

'Too long,' she said. She kissed him on his weathered cheek, then stepped back and gave Lawless an unfriendly glance. 'You are still alive, I see?'

'No thanks to you,' he said. 'Ridin' off an' leaving us like that.' Giving her no chance to respond, he turned to Nunez, adding: 'How come you never said you were her grandfather before — back there on the trail?'

'For her safety, *mi amigo*, we decided to keep it a secret. I have enemies who would gladly hurt me by harming Catarina.'

'That why she changed her name to Mateos?'

'It was not her but I who changed my name.'

'That's right, I forgot — when you quit bein' a *bandido*. So your real name is Mateos?'

Nunez nodded. 'This must never be spoken of outside this cave — agreed?' He included Tess as he spoke, and she nodded right away.

'You have my word,' she promised. 'In fact I've already forgotten it.'

'*Bueno*.'

'*Abuelo*,' Catarina pleaded, 'you must leave here — now — while the men are with El Flaco.'

Nunez nodded, then said to Tess: 'Your husband, señora — where is he?'

'When I left he was asleep,' she replied. 'He'd been drinking and — '

'She tells the truth,' Catarina said. 'The *gringo*, he is not in the big cave with the others.'

'What about you?' Lawless asked. 'You comin' with us?'

'I have no choice,' Catarina said. 'Once I have done this, my life here is over.'

15

As the four of them left the cave and quietly descended the rocky slope leading down to the valley floor, Lawless realized their horses were missing. Angry, he asked Catarina if she knew where they were. She didn't, but guessed the bandits had taken them, putting them with their own horses in the corral beyond the trees.

'Obviously El Flaco figures on keepin' us here,' Lawless said to Nunez.

The former bandit nodded. 'Our only chance is to get to the horses. Come. *Prisa*!'

Ducked low, they hurried into the trees. The trees were close together and their intertwined branches blocked out the moon, the darkness making it hard to see. Lawless stopped after they'd gone a short distance and gestured for the others to gather around him. He then turned to Tess, saying: 'Reckon you ought to come with us, Mrs. Albright.'

'I can't. My husband — '

'Forget your husband, ma'am. It's El Flaco you should be worryin' about. When he finds out we're gone, you could be in a pile of trouble.'

'He's right, señora,' Nunez said. 'For your own safety, you must come with us.'

'And leave Tuck behind?'

'From what I've seen,' Lawless said, eyeing her bruised face, 'you'd be better off without him.'

Tess's hand unconsciously strayed to her split and swollen lips. 'If I did go, Suarez would know I was involved. Then he may take his rage out on Tuck. No, much as I want to go with you, I can't.'

'I'm all for loyalty,' Lawless said, 'but if you don't mind me sayin', yours is misplaced. Hell, he'd leave you in a flash and never give it a second thought.'

'Possibly.'

'Try 'definitely.''

Tess shrugged, her voice unemotional as she said: 'Whether or not you're right, Mr. Lawless, doesn't really matter. At the altar, when I said 'For better or for worse,' I meant it. That's all there is to it.'

'That vow,' Lawless growled, 'did it include him beatin' you bloody every so often?'

Tess inhaled deeply, biting back any retort, and forced herself to say calmly: 'You'd better hurry, all of you. Every second you stand here talking only adds to your chances of getting caught.' Standing on tiptoe, she lightly kissed Lawless on the cheek. 'Thank you for everything.' Then including the others, she said: '*Paseo con Dios*.' She hurried off toward her cave before anyone could stop her.

'Damn,' Lawless breathed. 'I hate to run out on her like this.'

'If you stay,' Catarina warned, 'we'll all die. I guarantee it.'

Lawless knew she was right. 'Let's make some dust,' he said to Nunez. The former bandit smiled, relieved, and led the way through the trees.

They ran for about fifty yards, stumbling over roots in the darkness, and presently came to the far edge of the trees. Before them, lit by moonlight, was a large open area boxed in on three sides by sheer cliffs. It contained two corrals. One was filled with the *bandidos*' horses; the other held Lawless's pale gray stallion and the horse ridden by Nunez. The stallion was still saddled and Lawless, knowing how it must have tried to bite and kick anyone who came close to it, grinned despite the circumstances.

He then quietly asked Catarina if she knew where lookouts might be posted. There were none, she said. Not here. The only lookouts were the ones on the cliffs guarding the entrance to the canyon. Since there was no other way in or out, El Flaco felt there was no need for more lookouts.

Lawless grudgingly had to agree with him. 'Mount up,' he told Nunez. Then to Catarina: 'Open the other gate and we'll cut you out a horse before we stampede the others.'

She dismissed his offer with a withering look and hurried to the corral containing the bandits' horses.

Lawless looked at Nunez, who shrugged. 'Forgive her rudeness, *mi amigo*. If I had raised her, she would know the meaning of manners.'

'No need to apologize,' Lawless said. 'I like a woman with sand.' He watched Catarina vault over the fence and move among the nervous, shifting horses, silently admiring her; then he opened the gate to the other corral and approached the stallion. It bared its teeth at him, and swung around so it could kick him with its hind legs.

'Try it,' Lawless warned, 'an' I swear to God, hoss, I'll put a round 'tween your goddamn eyes.'

The Spanish purebred may not have understood him, but it heard the threat in his tone and obediently came to a standstill. Lawless eyed it suspiciously for a moment, not fully trusting the stallion, and then stepped up into the saddle.

Nunez, already mounted, rode out of the gate and reined up by the other corral. Inside, Catarina had already swung up onto the back of a leggy sorrel mare and with one hand clutching its long mane, was guiding it through the herd toward her grandfather. Nunez opened the gate for her and then signaled to Lawless, who rode to the rear of the other corral.

There, he waited until Nunez and Catarina were in the clear and then fired several shots into the air.

Instantly, the horses panicked. Whinnying with fear, they charged the open gate. There were too many of them to get through it at once, but their combined weight and momentum knocked over the fence on either side of the gate, allowing them to burst free and stampede off into the night.

Lawless, Nunez and Catarina rode behind the rear of the frightened horses, urging them ever faster with shouts and gunfire.

The whole canyon echoed with the thunder of their hooves as they raced toward the opening between the steep cliffs.

Alerted by the noise, El Flaco and his men burst out of the large cave. The panicked horses raced past them, followed by Lawless, Nunez and Catarina.

Immediately, the bandits began firing at them. But it was no turkey shoot. Lawless and his companions, ducked low over their speeding horses, presented no easy target. Clouds of dust kicked up by the stampeding herd swirled around them, adding to the bandits' problem, and every bullet missed.

Atop the cliffs on either side of the entrance-exit the lookouts peered down into the darkness, trying to pick out something to shoot at. But it was even harder from above and the few shots they did try weren't even close.

Once out of the canyon, into the open scrubland, the horses gradually slowed down. Lawless fired a few shots over their heads to keep them going, but soon the herd split up into groups and disappeared into the darkness.

Lawless reined up beside Nunez and his granddaughter, who were looking back toward the canyon.

'We got at least an hour or so before they can round up their horses,' Lawless said. 'We'll be long gone by then.'

Catarina sighed, resigned. 'It does not end here. El Flaco will find us, no matter where we try to hide. He has to or he will lose face in the eyes of his men — and he cannot let this happen. There are those among them, enemies who are just waiting for him to falter so they can take over.'

'Let him come,' Lawless said grimly.

'Once we're across the border, I'll make it easy for him to find me. An' when he does, I'll make sure he has more to worry about than just losing control of his men.'

16

They rode hard for several hours and then stopped to rest and water the horses. A desert wind had sprung up and it turned bone-chilling cold. Earlier the moon had gone behind the clouds, bringing darkness to the desert scrubland, and coyotes could be heard yip-yipping in the distance.

Everyone was tired but Lawless insisted they push on, claiming that it was their only hope of keeping the bandits at a distance. What about the horses, Nunez said. Lawless shrugged. 'We'll rest 'em every hour or so. With water and a little grain, hopefully we can keep them fresh enough to reach the border before El Flaco and his men catch up to us.'

'I've got a better idea,' Catarina said. 'I have friends in a village less than two hours' ride from here. If I ask them, they will hide us until morning — '

'What about El Flaco and his men?'

'There is bad blood between them. I doubt if El Flaco would go there to look for us.'

'An' if he does?' Lawless asked.

'The villagers wouldn't betray us, of that I'm sure. Then, come sunup, with our horses well-rested, we can easily reach the border without stopping.'

'What do you think?' Lawless asked Nunez.

'I am not against resting, *mi amigo*. And if my granddaughter says it is safe, then I believe her.'

Lawless shrugged. 'Lead the way,' he told Catarina.

A dust storm was blowing when they reached the village of *Vientos de Dios*. So small it was not shown on any map, it consisted of a scattering of weathered adobe buildings and sun-bleached shacks that were flanked on the east and south by a range of steep sandstone cliffs and by seemingly

endless miles of sun-scorched waste-
land on the north and west.

There were no streets, only numer-
ous narrow paths that had been carved
out of the earth by dangerous, seasonal
flash floods, the red dirt rutted and
baked hard as stone by the relentless
broiling sun.

With kerchiefs protecting the lower
half of their faces from the flying dust,
the three riders entered what appeared
to be an abandoned village. Catarina
led them through the darkness to a
two-story pale-blue cantina that sat on
a corner, facing the main street —
which was nothing more than a trail
that meandered uninterrupted through
town and on out into the desert. Above
the front door the name of the cantina
had long since been eaten away by the
Winds of God, which besides lending
their name to the village usually
manifested themselves as howling dust
storms.

Ducked low over their mounts, they
rode around in back of the cantina and

dismounted beside two crumbling adobe walls, which was all that remained of a stable. The walls, though no taller than Lawless, offered some shelter from the storm; and removing their kerchiefs, they soaked them with water from Lawless's canteen and then dampened the sand-caked muzzles of the horses.

'What about the saddles?' Nunez asked as he wiped the dust from his eyes.

'We'll take 'em off later — *after* we decide if it's safe to stay here. No offense,' Lawless added as Catarina glared at him. 'But I ain't stayed alive all these years by takin' chances.'

They entered the little candle-lit cantina. Inside, its thick walls hid most of the noise of storm. There were only three other customers — *campasinos*, their skin wrinkled and burned black by the sun, their white cotton clothing smeared with honest dirt as they sat hunched over at a table wolfing down tortillas, beans and rice. They turned, startled, as the door suddenly opened, then was blown inward by the howling wind so that it slammed against the wall.

Instantly, all but one of the candles were blown out.

Lawless, Nunez and Catarina were blown in by the wind, stumbling forward as if a giant hand had pushed them from behind. Recovering first, Lawless quickly grabbed the door and after a fight managed to close it. At once quiet returned to the cantina. The field hands went on eating and the large fleshy man behind the bar, after sizing up his new customers, decided they were not threatening and moved about the room relighting the candles.

'*Buenas noches, señors,*' he began — then stopped, happily surprised as he recognized Catarina. 'Señorita Mateos, it is good to see you again!'

'Good to see you too, Ramon.' Catarina hurried to greet the barkeep, who came around from behind the bar and gave her a fond hug. They spoke briefly about how many months it had been since they last saw each other, then Catarina introduced Lawless and Nunez, calling them both close friends. 'We could all use a beer, Ramon,' she added, 'then I'd like to talk to you alone for a few minutes.'

'*Con mucho gusto*,' Ramon Rega said. He went back behind the bar and served the three of them beer in tall red clay mugs. Each took a long swallow, then closed their eyes and sighed with satisfaction as the beer cooled their parched throats.

'I'll be right back,' Catarina told Lawless and Nunez. Setting her mug down, she followed Ramon into a back room.

As if it were a signal the three *campasinos* got up, placed coins on the table, donned their straw sombreros and started for the door. Wanting no trouble, they kept their heads down and did not look at Lawless or Nunez as they passed.

Lawless watched them leave. He then

gulped down his beer, wiped the froth from his mouth with his sleeve and said to Nunez: 'I got a bad feelin' about this, *amigo.*'

'*De que manera?*'

'I dunno. My gut just tells me we shouldn't be here.'

'In this storm,' Nunez said, finishing his beer, 'anywhere is better than outside.'

Lawless didn't say anything.

'You do not trust my granddaughter?'

'I didn't say that.'

'But do you?'

'Much as I trust anyone — no, that's not true. I'd trust you with my life. But you're on a real short list.'

' — which does not include Catarina?'

Lawless shrugged apologetically. 'I'm a suspicious bastard, *amigo.* Takes me a mighty long time 'fore I fully trust someone.' He broke off as Catarina and Ramon returned.

'There are rooms upstairs we can use,' she explained as Ramon continued on into the kitchen.

'Did you tell him El Flaco an' his men are doggin' our trail?' Lawless asked.

'*Si*. He doesn't think they will come here, but said even if they do it won't matter. The storm will cover our tracks and no one will betray us.'

'What about our horses?'

'Ramon said he'd unsaddle them and hide them somewhere they cannot be seen and then bring us food.'

'They need to be watered and grained, too.'

'He'll take care of that. Stop worrying,' she said, seeing Lawless's frown. 'I explained everything to him. He promised to post lookouts.'

Lawless turned to Nunez, saying: 'One of us should stay awake while the others sleep. Just in case.'

'It must be you or Catarina,' the former bandit said. He yawned and rubbed the stiffness from his lower back. 'Sleep is stealing my eyes.'

'Reckon it's been a long day for all of

us,' Lawless said, adding: 'I'll take the first watch. You two get some rest. I'll wake one of you when I get sleepy.'

'Come, *mi abuelo*,' Catarina said, grasping her grandfather's arm, 'I will show you where to sleep.' She led him to the stairs leading up to the rooms.

Lawless entered the greasy little kitchen and joined Ramon at the wood-burning stove. 'Sure could use some coffee, *amigo*.'

Ramon took a mug from a shelf and waddled fatly to the blackened coffee-pot sitting on the stove. '*Un momento, señor*. I will make fresh for you.'

'*Gracias*. But I'll drink what's in the pot. Believe me, *hombre*, it can't be no worse than the coffee I've made over the years.'

* * *

Nothing eventful happened during the night. An hour or so before dawn the storm died, leaving the sky muddy and

141

the warm morning air choked with settling dust.

Weary, Lawless waked Catarina and asked her to take over for him. Though still half-asleep, she agreed without argument, dressed and told him to use her bed rather than risk disturbing her grandfather. He obeyed, insisting that she wake him after two hours, and was asleep moments after he stretched out on the mattress.

The next thing he remembered, Catarina was shaking him out of his sleep and offering him a mug of fresh coffee. She added that Ramon's wife, Marta, was fixing breakfast and there was water behind the cantina for him to wash up.

Outside, the water in the chipped earthen bowl was hot and after washing away the sweat-caked dust, Lawless dried himself on his shirt-tail, finished his hand-rolled and ground it out under his heel. He squinted up at the still-muddy sky, then at the flat empty scrubland stretched out before him. In the windless air he could just make out the distant cliffs and canyon ridges to the east and south, their color the same pale yellow as the rising sun.

Despite lack of sleep, he felt surprisingly good. He knew he'd feel even better if he shaved, but wasn't comfortable wasting precious time on something that wasn't necessary. Dumping the dirty water, which the thirsty sand sucked up immediately, he carried the bowl inside.

Nunez and Catarina sat at one of the tables, already halfway through their *huevos rancheros*. The delicious smell of corn tortillas and fried eggs cooked with salsa reminded Lawless just how famished he was and he wolfed his food down without saying a word. Then rolling a smoke he finished his coffee and thanked Marta for her hospitality. A big-breasted, big-hipped *mestiza* with lank black hair and expressive black eyes, she was pregnant with Ramon's seventh child. She smiled a lot but said little. She made it clear though that she was disappointed Lawless didn't want more food, and as she returned to the kitchen with his empty plate muttered something in Spanish that Lawless didn't understand but which made Ramon, Catarina and Nunez laugh.

'Okay, what'd she just say about me?' he asked them.

'That for such a tall man you have the appetite of a *gorrion*,' Nunez said.

'Do I want to know what a *gorrion* is?'

'Somewhere 'tween a corpse and a coyote skeleton.'

'Glad she thinks so highly of me,' Lawless said.

Catarina laughed. 'Forgive my grandfather's humor,' she said. 'A *gorrion* is a sparrow.'

Lawless patted his full belly and chuckled. 'Well, all I can say is sparrows in Mexico must eat a damn sight more than their cousins in Texas — ' He broke off as the door flew open and a villager hurried in. He looked alarmed and spoke rapidly to Nunez, who

144

nodded and sent him back out.

'El Flaco?' Lawless said, buckling on his gun-belt.

'No. Sanchez has never seen these men before — or the señorita who leads them.'

'Señorita?'

Nunez nodded. '*Si. Una mujer muy hermosa.*'

Lawless had a sinking feeling as he rose and hurried to the door.

'You are expecting someone?'

'Always,' Lawless replied. Opening the door a crack, he peered out and saw a column of heavily armed Mexican riders approaching. All rode finely bred black horses. All the men were dressed alike, all sat astride *charro* saddles and all wore black high-crowned sombreros. They were led by a young, strikingly attractive Castilian woman in richly embroidered riding clothes, a ruffled white blouse, hand-tooled boots and an extravagantly large, flat-crowned black hat with a plaited drawstring dangling under her chin.

Lawless expelled his worst fears in a loud sigh.

Nunez moved up behind him and peered over his shoulder. '*Quien es ella?*'

'Delfina Vargas,' Lawless said grimly.

'The governor's daughter? What is she doing here?'

'Lookin' for me.' Lawless said, adding: 'Stay here, *amigo*. You too,' he told Catarina. 'This ain't your fight.'

'Wait! Come with me, señor,' Ramon urged. 'I will hide you until they are gone.'

Lawless shook his head. 'They'd only burn your village down an' torture you an' your friends, or their children, until someone told them where I was.'

Knowing he was right, Ramon fell silent.

'To have found you here of all places,' Nunez said glumly, 'this is indeed the worst kind of luck.'

'Luck had nothin' to do with it,' Lawless said, staring at Catarina. 'Did it?'

'What are you suggesting?' she said, flaring. 'That I told them?'

'Who else?'

'No, no, you are mistaken,' began Nunez.

'How could I tell anyone anything?' Catarina said angrily. 'I have not left your side since leaving El Flaco's camp.'

'Didn't have to,' Lawless said. 'You sent a rider *before* we left — someone you could trust — informing Governor Vargas that you'd bring us here, to *Vientos de Dios*, for the night. Then you persuaded us to — '

'Why would I do that?' she demanded. 'I do not know the governor or his daughter.'

'Maybe not. But this is a hell of a way to introduce yourself — to make a name for yourself so that if and when there is a revolution, you'll be in favor with the man funding it.'

'Catarina?' Nunez said, turning to his granddaughter. 'Say this is not true. Tell me that you would never betray a man who is my friend?'

'Save your breath,' Lawless said as Catarina wouldn't look her grandfather in the eyes. 'What's done is done. Reckon it's for the best anyway. Now I don't have to spend the rest of my life lookin' over my shoulder. *Adios, mi amigo*,' he added to Nunez — and stepped out into the morning sunlight.

17

On seeing him Delfina raised her hand, and the men behind her reined up but kept their rifles trained on Lawless.

Delfina nudged her elegant purebred horse forward until she was directly in front of Lawless, then she too reined up and sat there, straight-backed and proud, studying him.

'You have been a difficult man to find, Lawless.'

'I've done my best,' he said, adding: 'How's your father?'

Delfina's lips tightened angrily for a moment and her dark eyes blazed with fire. Then she controlled herself and in perfect English, taught to her by a succession of British governesses, said: 'As always, he is anxious to hang you.'

'An' you, *princesa* — how anxious are you to see a rope around my neck?'

'You will find out soon enough.' Her

voice was husky and passionate and contained a sting of contempt. 'Take him,' she told her men.

Before they could obey, Lawless jerked his iron, the big Colt seeming to leap into his hand, and aimed it at Delfina.

'I may hang,' he said quietly, 'but you won't live to see it.'

She showed no fear. She didn't even blink. 'If you must shoot me, *querida*, pull the trigger. But it will not save your life.'

For an instant Lawless didn't wilt. Then he chuckled, lowered the hammer and holstered his Colt.

'You know me too well, *princesa*.'

'Do not call me that,' she snapped. 'I hate that word — almost as much as I hate you.' She backed her horse up, and two of her men dismounted and bound Lawless's arms to his sides with ropes.

'*Alto!*'

Nunez and Catarina stepped out of the cantina, rifles aimed at Delfina and her men.

'Release him,' Nunez told Delfina.

She ignored them. To Lawless, she said: 'Tell these fools to go back inside or my men will kill them.'

'Do as she says,' Lawless told Nunez. 'You can't help me. An' you'll only get killed tryin'.'

'Perhaps,' Nunez said. 'But I would get satisfaction out of knowing others died with me.'

'I wouldn't,' Lawless said. 'And I sure as hell don't want to be responsible for your granddaughter gettin' killed. Now please, do as I ask, old friend. Both of you . . . go back inside.'

Nunez hesitated. Then grudgingly, he lowered his rifle and nodded at Catarina to do the same. She obeyed and they glumly returned to the cantina.

'What, now?' Lawless asked Delfina.

She turned to a young handsome man, Fernando, mounted nearby. 'Give him your horse.'

He obeyed without hesitation. Dismounting, he helped Lawless step up into the saddle and then swung up behind one of the other men.

Delfina spurred her horse forward, Lawless alongside her, and together they and her men rode out of the village.

18

A mile or so south of the village Delfina reined up beside a large rocky outcrop and ordered her men to keep watch. She then told Lawless to dismount. When he did, she ordered Fernando to untie Lawless.

'But, señora — '

'Do it!'

Fernando obeyed, muttering: '*Esto no complacer a su padre.*'

'Would it please my father more if I told him you keep trying to kiss me?'

Fernando blanched.

'Now, give me your *pistola*.'

He reluctantly handed her his pistol.

'All of you,' she told the men, 'stay here while I deal with this *gringo*.' She then pressed the pistol against Lawless's ribs and forced him to walk ahead of her, around behind the rocks.

As they walked Lawless said over his

shoulder: 'I see you still have that magic touch with men.'

Delfina wasn't amused. 'At least they do not desert me.'

'I didn't desert you,' Lawless grumbled. 'I was run out of town by your father, His Majesty, the governor.'

Delfina smiled despite herself. ''His Majesty'? It is a description that fits Papa.'

'Much better than 'señora' fits you.'

She sighed, pushed her hat back off her head so that her long black hair fell loosely about her exquisite oval face, and leaned back against the rocks.

'I am married by name only.'

'Another order from the throne, huh?'

She shrugged, dismissing his question. Then she draped her arms about his neck and offered up her mouth to him.

'Que pasa?' she said when he didn't respond. 'Don't you want to kiss me?'

'More'n anything. But — '

She silenced him by pressing her lips over his.

He started to resist, then gave in and

154

put everything he felt into the kiss.

Delfina broke away first with a faint gasp and then smiled, pleased with herself.

'If that was to remind me about what I'm missin',' Lawless said, 'you can save your passion. I already knew.'

'Yet you never came back to me?'

'Your father's watchdogs saw to that.'

'You were never afraid of my father — or his watchdogs.'

'Maybe I finally figured out that gettin' killed wasn't love's answer.'

'Ahh,' she taunted, 'the wisdom that comes with age.'

'I like to call it maturity.'

'And now that I am here,' Delfina said, again draping her arms around his neck, 'will that 'maturity' stop you from coming to be with me in Chihuahua?'

'Reckon your father might have somethin' to say 'bout that — your father *and* your husband.'

Again she dismissed his remark with a shrug. 'They are both in Mexico,' she said, using the Mexican term for

155

Mexico City, 'on business.'

'How convenient.'

Then, when she didn't say anything: 'So you rode all the way up here to find me?'

'Do not flatter yourself, *querido*. The truth is I only came for the horse.'

Lawless frowned, surprised. 'Alano? But he was a gift.'

'Gifts can be returned.'

'Not this one.'

'I can always order my men to ride back to the village and take him.'

'They'll have to kill me first.'

'I do not want that.'

'Makes two of us.'

Delfina studied Lawless, obviously still in love with him. Then reality crept in and she sighed, resigned, and said: 'I cannot defy my father, even if I wanted to.'

'An' you don't, right?'

'One day perhaps — not now. There is too much at stake for me.'

'Like what — ridin' on the coat-tails of Papa's revolution?'

Delfina tried to hide her surprise.

'Don't act like you don't know what I'm talkin' about,' Lawless said. 'Ain't a body in Mexico doesn't know he wants to be president.'

'Then you must know you cannot fight me on this.'

Lawless grinned sourly. 'Reckon you've forgotten how stubborn I am.'

Delfina sighed, and said: 'Please, *querido*, let me have Alano. It is a matter of principle with him.'

'Sorry. No deal.'

'I'll give you another stallion — one that is equally pure and beautiful.'

'What's the point? Sooner or later your father would find out about it, and then that horse would become a 'matter of principle' too.' He suddenly pulled her hard against him and kissed her with everything he had. Then he pushed her away, saying: 'If you're goin' to shoot me, *princesa*, better get to it.'

'*Usted es un necio!*' she said, raising the pistol.

But of course he already knew that.

19

The gunshot that shattered the silence behind the rocks brought smiles to the men gathered on the trail by their horses.

'What did I tell you?' Fernando bragged to them. 'This *gringo* pig meant nothing to Señora Vargas. She told me so herself last night.'

The men laughed derisively.

'His death will not open her bedroom door for you, *chico*. Not even in your grandest dreams.'

They all laughed again, infuriating the young man.

'You will see,' he said hotly. 'One night when the señora is lonely, her arms will open and she will — '

'Will what?' Delfina said, approaching from behind the rocks.

Fernando blushed, avoided her angry stare and said nothing.

'I asked you a question,' she said, aiming the pistol at him. 'Answer me or I'll shoot you as I did the *gringo*.'

Fernando stammered, his words too jumbled to make sense, and dropped to his knees. '*Por favor, perdoname, señora.*'

Delfina didn't answer. Rage had drained the color from her beautiful face. She seemed about to shoot him. But at the last instant she put her boot on the back of his neck and forced his head down until his face was squashed in the dirt.

'I ought to kill you as my father would,' she said. 'But you are not worthy of a bullet.' Removing her boot from his neck, she swung her heel sideways, raking the six-pointed rowel of her gilded spur across his face, drawing blood.

Fernando screamed and clutched at his bleeding cheek.

Delfina stabbed her gloved finger at him. 'Get out of Chihuahua! If I ever see you again, I will have you butchered with machetes. *Me entiendes?*'

'*Si, señora . . . si . . . si . . .* '

'*Bueno.*' She walked to her horse, mounted, wheeled it around and rode off.

The men quickly swung up into their saddles and galloped after her, leaving Fernando standing there, bleeding and without a horse.

* * *

Not long after Delfina and her men had left, Nunez and Catarina rode out of the village and back along the trail in search of Lawless's corpse. Halfway to the rocks, they saw Fernando walking toward them, one hand clutching a blood-soaked kerchief to his slashed cheek.

'If you're looking for the *gringo*,' he said as they reined up beside him, 'you will find his body behind those rocks.' He pointed at the rocky outcrop and Nunez and Catarina exchanged dismayed looks.

'Who killed him?' Nunez asked.

'Señora Vargas — with my *pistola*.' Before they could question him further, Fernando glumly continued on along the trail.

Heavy-hearted, Nunez and his grand-daughter kicked up their horses and headed for the rocks.

But before they reached them, a familiar figure appeared from behind the rocks. Recognizing Lawless, they waved and joyously galloped toward him.

Equally pleased to see them, Lawless stopped and waited for them.

'*Madre de Dios*, this is a miracle!' Nunez exclaimed as they dismounted beside him. 'I cannot believe you are still alive, *mi amigo*!'

'Me, neither,' Lawless said.

'The man we just passed,' Catarina said, pointing off at Fernando, 'he thinks you are dead.'

'There was a moment back there when I thought I was too,' Lawless said. 'Guess it wasn't in the cards.'

Catarina eyed him with a glint of jealousy. 'Señora Vargas, she must love you very much.'

Lawless grunted. 'Once, maybe. Not so much now.'

'Why else would she let you live?'

''cause it suits her. If it didn't, believe me I'd be lyin' in my own blood right now.'

'Be grateful you are not.'

'Gratitude has a price — 'specially when there's a Vargas attached to it.'

Catarina shook her head at him. 'If I should ever save your life, Lawless, I hope you will speak more kindly of me.'

'Depends on the reason you saved it.'

Jealousy again flared in Catarina's dark, fierce eyes. 'And Señora Vargas — what was her reason?'

Nunez glared at his granddaughter. '*Nieta* — what you ask is not your business.'

'It's okay, I don't mind tellin' her,' Lawless said. Then to Catarina: 'She wanted me to come to Chihuahua City an' share her bed.'

'What about her husband?' Catarina demanded. 'He will not mind this?'

'Seems he spends a lot of time in Mexico City.'

Nunez sighed wistfully. 'She is a most beautiful woman. A man would be *loco* not to enjoy the fruit while it is ripe.'

Lawless chuckled. 'Well, while you're dreamin' of enjoyin' fruit, *amigo*, I'm goin' back to the village to pick up my horse. I've still got some unfinished business to take care of.'

'*Como que?*'

'Mrs. Albright.'

'What about her?' Catarina said suspiciously.

Lawless hesitated, as if trying to find a suitable answer, then said: 'This probably don't make a hill of sense. But I came down here to find the Albrights and take 'em back to New Mexico.'

'But you did find them,' Nunez reminded.

'Yeah, but they're still here an' I don't believe in leavin' a job half-finished.'

Nunez looked alarmed. 'You are going back to Cañon de Muchas Cuevas?'

'Soon as I get my horse.'

'You can't be serious,' Catarina said. 'El Flaco will kill you!'

'Possibly.'

'Even if you are lucky enough to survive,' put in Nunez, 'Señora Albright will not leave without her husband. She said as much.'

'Then I reckon I'll have to bring him along, too.'

'You talk like a fool,' Catarina said angrily. 'Señor Albright will not leave, not under any condition. Or have you forgotten that he and El Flaco are plotting to start a revolution?'

'I haven't forgotten anythin',' Lawless said.

'Then I am confused,' Nunez said. 'How can one man — even you Lawless — expect to pull off this madness against so many?'

''cause this time, *amigo*, I'm goin' to have help — a whole bunch of help.'

Catarina, who'd been glaring at him

164

in silence, suddenly exclaimed: 'Señora Vargas!'

Lawless didn't respond, but there was no denial in his light gray eyes.

His silent admission enraged Catarina. '*Bastardo*!' she hissed.

Nunez looked horrified. '*Silencio* — '

'No, I will not keep quiet,' she raged. Then to Lawless: 'You planned this! You risked my grandfather's life for no reason — '

He stopped her. 'You don't think I know that? Hell, woman, it's gnawin' a hole in my belly.' He turned to Nunez, adding: 'Sorry, old friend. I didn't mean it to turn out like this.'

Nunez smiled wearily. 'There is no need for apologies between *compadres*.'

Catarina gave Lawless and her grandfather a disgusted look. '*Hombres*!' she said bitterly. '*Tu me vuelves loco*.' Vaulting into the saddle, she spurred her horse away.

Lawless and Nunez looked after her for a moment, then at each other, then after Catarina again.

Nunez sighed. 'Being a grandfather can be most difficult.'

'So I'm beginnin' to learn,' Lawless said. He helped Nunez get mounted, then swung up behind him.

They rode at an easy lope in the direction of the village.

'I have great love for my granddaughter,' Nunez continued, as if thinking aloud. 'But I would be lying if I did not admit she can be most exasperating at times.'

'That,' Lawless said wryly, 'is puttin' it mildly.'

20

Ramon and many of the villagers were gathered outside the cantina when Lawless and Nunez rode up. But as they dismounted, and Lawless looked around, he could see no sign of Catarina.

Ramon pumped his hand. 'I am glad you are safe, señor,' he said, and led him over to his horse. The purebred Spanish stallion was tied to the hitch-rail, snorting and nervously pawing at the dirt.

'He is grained and well-rested,' Ramon said, 'as I promised Catarina.'

'*Gracias*,' Lawless said, eyeing the stallion. 'He give you much trouble?'

'None, señor. At first he show me his teeth. But then, after he understand I mean him no harm, he was fine.'

'I've seen those teeth a few times myself,' Lawless said. He dug some coins from his jeans. 'Here, I 'preciate your help.'

Ramon looked offended. 'No, no, señor. I do this only because you are a friend of Catarina's.'

'Well, thanks anyway,' Lawless said, pocketing the money. 'Next time I'm down this way, I'll be sure'n stop by for tequila. Where is she by the way? I'd like to say goodbye.'

Ramon looked unhappy. 'Catarina is with my wife, señor. But she will not talk to you. This she tell me many times.'

'Women,' Lawless said disgustedly. 'They stab you in the back then act like you're to blame. I swear they're more trouble than they're worth.'

'*Es la voluntad de Dios*,' Ramon said.

'If it is,' Lawless grumbled, 'then the rumor's right: God *is* a woman.' He stepped into the stirrup — then quickly jerked his foot loose and jumped back as the stallion took a swipe at him. 'Try that again, you sonofabitch,' he warned, 'an' I'll sell you to the Apaches.'

The pale gray stallion snorted and

faced front. Lawless cautiously stepped into the stirrup again and then, when the horse ignored him, swung up into the saddle. Then wheeling the horse around, he rode up to Nunez, who was answering the villagers' questions.

'So long,' he said, reaching down to grasp Nunez's hand. 'See you around sometime.'

'*Via con Dios, mi amigo* . . . ' Nunez held Lawless's callused hand fondly for a moment, then let go and sadly watched as his friend rode off.

★ ★ ★

He'd been riding for a while through open desert, the sun hot on his back, when he heard hoof-beats behind him. He reined up, twisted around and saw a distant rider galloping along the trail toward him.

''Be damned,' he muttered. He stood up in the stirrups to stretch his legs, then sat down, hooked one leg over the saddle horn, took out the fixings and rolled a smoke. Sealing the paper with his tongue, he put the cigarette between his lips, flared a match on his jeans and lit up. He inhaled deeply, enjoying the taste of tobacco, and settled down to wait.

He'd just taken the last drag and flipped the butt away when the rider pulled up alongside him.

Their gazes locked. Neither spoke. Neither looked away.

If Lawless had expected her to be contrite, or apologetic in any way, he saw no sign of it in her defiant expression. If anything, her look suggested that she was doing him a favor just by being here and he should be damned glad to see her.

Finally, he said: 'What're you doin' here?'

'*Mi abuelo me dijo que le ayudar.*'

'I don't need your help.'

Catarina looked long and hard at him as if trying to make a decision. Then she said quietly: 'I did not betray you as you think.'

Lawless scoffed. 'No? Then what do you call it? Or do you think I'm dumb enough to believe that Delfina showin' up with her men was just a coincidence?'

'Believe what you wish. You will anyway.' She turned her horse around, ready to leave.

He grabbed her reins, stopping her. 'No, no, you can't wriggle out of it that easy. Either you told her where I was or you didn't — which was it?'

Catarina didn't answer for a long moment. Then she sighed and, meeting his angry stare, said: 'It's true. I did send someone to tell Señora Vargas where you'd be. But I did not do it to betray you.'

'Could've fooled me.'

'It's the truth. It was the only way I could be sure that she'd come and help you.'

Lawless laughed mirthlessly. 'Help me — to do what?'

'Take Señora Albright away from her husband.'

171

Lawless frowned, confused. 'I don't follow.'

Catarina paused, searching for the right words. Then: 'I am not who you think I am.'

'Right now, considerin' what I think of you, that's a good thing. Okay,' he added when she didn't continue. 'Who are you?'

'I am with the Federal Police.'

Lawless almost laughed. 'The *Federales*? Jesus, woman, you really expect me to believe that?'

Her tight-lipped expression said she did.

'Then what the hell were you doin' with El Flaco and his men? Or didn't you know they were *bandidos*?'

'Of course I knew,' she said, ignoring his sarcasm. 'It is the reason I was there.'

''fraid you've lost me.'

'Orders.'

'Whose orders?'

'*El Presidente's*.'

'President Diaz told you to be a bandit?'

'Course not. But he spoke to my superiors. Said he'd heard rumors that El Flaco and a *gringo* named Tucker Albright were plotting to overthrow him and he had to know if it was true.'

Lawless looked into Catarina's dark, fearless eyes and saw nothing but sincerity.

'Let me get this straight,' he said soberly. 'You became a bandit in order to spy on El Flaco — to find out if he and Tucker Albright were stirrin' up the locals against President Diaz?'

'*Si.*'

'Why a woman, not a man?'

'It is well-known that El Flaco prefers the company of women to men.'

'Uh-*huh.*'

'I would still be there, too, if you and my grandfather had not showed up.'

Her anger was too convincing, Lawless realized, for her to be lying. Mind churning, he said: 'And now you're willin' to risk your life to help me get Mrs. Albright out of there? Why?'

'Because she is innocent . . . has no idea that her husband is involved in Mexican politics.'

'Even if that's true, what's that to you?'

'Personally, nothing. But she is a *Norteamericano*. Should anything bad happen to her — or, God forbid, she gets killed — then your government will blame President Diaz and right now, he needs allies not more enemies.'

It made sense, Lawless had to admit. But there was something else that didn't.

'All right,' he said, 'let's say I believe you. There's still a hole in your story.'

'Señora Vargas?'

'Exactly. I mean if all you've said is true, then why would she help me? As a *Federale*, you must know that her father has agreed to fund the revolution. So why would she help anyone who's against the governor? And she *has* already agreed to help me.'

'I know.'

He frowned, surprised. 'How do you

know? You weren't behind those rocks when we cut our deal.'

Catarina smiled thinly. 'I didn't have to be. I am a woman. She is a woman. When a woman truly loves a man, she will do almost anything to keep him at her side. And once you're in Chihuahua, close to her, the señora believes you won't be able to resist her.'

Lawless hated to admit it, but inwardly he knew she was right.

21

It was mid-afternoon when they approached the Cañon de Muches Cuevas. Still a half-mile away, they stopped to rest the horses and drink from their canteens, their eyes searching the distant cliff-tops for lookouts.

'Where did Señora Vargas say she would meet you?' Catarina asked.

'At the entrance.' Lawless trained his field glasses on the V-shaped opening between the two towering sandstone cliffs but saw no one. '*Nada*.'

'Perhaps she decided to ride ahead to warn El Flaco not to shoot you?'

Lawless shrugged. 'Possibly. Like *El Presidente*, Governor Vargas wouldn't want to alienate the U.S. by killing an American. Washington hears about it, they might send troops to help Diaz and together they'd crush the revolution before it got started.' Returning the glasses to his saddlebag, he nudged the stallion onward.

Catarina followed, one hand holding the reins, the other resting on the butt of the nickel-plated pistol tucked in her belt.

When they were within a hundred yards of the canyon, they could see the heads of the lookouts perched atop the cliffs. But since they made no attempt to shoot or stop them, Lawless continued to ride slowly toward the entrance.

As they got closer, the lookouts stood up so Lawless and Catarina could see them. One, a short bearded man with a gray sombrero, motioned with his rifle for them to come ahead.

Hoping it wasn't a trap, Lawless led Catarina into the canyon. High above them on either side of the sheer cliffs, other lookouts waved them on. Lawless realized then that Catarina was right: Delfina must have arrived ahead of them and managed to convince El Flaco not to harm them.

'Reckon I owe you an apology, Cat.'

'Why?'

'I shouldn't have doubted you. The way they're treatin' us, only thing missing is a red carpet.'

'Let's hope they are as friendly on our way out,' she said. 'Knowing El Flaco like I do, I've learned he can change his mind faster than winter weather.'

Something greasy turned over in Lawless's stomach — something that he hadn't known existed before.

'How well *did* you know him?' he asked, at the same time wondering why he cared.

'*Bastante bien.*'

'Pretty good? — that doesn't tell me much.'

Catarina shrugged. 'It is all I can tell you.'

Irked, Lawless started to press her for details. Then, sensing it wouldn't get him anywhere, he gritted his teeth and kept quiet. But his interest in her wouldn't die. And as they continued along the trail, the little voice kept nagging at him and he again wondered why her relationship with a bandit mattered to him.

They rode on in silence — save for the hawks screeching as they circled high overhead.

'No,' Catarina said suddenly.

Lawless looked at her, surprised. 'No, what?'

'El Flaco did not bed me — if that's what you are wondering.'

'Never crossed my mind,' Lawless lied.

'I am glad. I would not want you to get the wrong impression of me.'

'Mean as a spy — a *Federale* — or a beautiful, devious woman?' he said, straight-faced.

'All three,' she replied. 'After all, if we are to become husband and wife, there should be no secrets between us.' Kicking her horse up, she rode on ahead of him toward the trees, her laughter echoing off the cliffs flanking them.

As they rode out of the trees together, on across the grassy meadow toward the caves, they were met by a dozen or more heavily armed *bandidos*. Blocking their path, the men trained their rifles on the intruders.

Catarina spoke rapidly to them in Spanish, and though Lawless did not understand everything she said, he grasped enough to know that she was telling them to move aside so they could talk to El Flaco.

The man who appeared to be the leader, a large, flaccid, swaggering man whom Catarina addressed as Hector, threatened them with his rifle and sullenly ordered them to drop their weapons and raise their hands.

'Ignore him,' she told Lawless. 'He is nothing but *un bolsa grande de viento*.'

'Maybe so,' Lawless said. 'But that 'big bag of wind' just happens to be pointin' a rifle right at my belly.'

Catarina scoffed and kicked up her

horse. She rode straight at Hector — so that he had to jump back out of her way or get ridden down.

'C'mon, *el pollo*,' she yelled derisively at Lawless. 'At least pretend you have a spine!'

The bandits laughed and all but Hector lowered their rifles.

Lawless, one eye on Hector, one hand on his holstered Colt, rode slowly past the men after Catarina.

She waited for him to catch up with her.

'Thanks for the compliment,' he said sourly.

'*De nada*,' she replied, eyes bright with laughter. 'But I warn you, *hombre*, when you meet El Flaco, you must show more courage.'

'Don't worry 'bout me,' Lawless said. '*Tengo mucho repollo*.'

She chuckled and dismounted, saying: 'In future I think it is better you speak only English.'

'Why?' he said, dismounting beside her.

'Because you just said you have much cabbage.' Handing her reins to one of the armed bandits standing guard outside the entrance, she marched into the cave ahead of Lawless.

22

A bandit with a long, greasy gunfighter mustache took away their weapons, and then led them into the cave where Delfina sat talking with El Flaco and his lieutenants. Other bandits, armed with rifles, pistols and machetes, sat or stood in groups nearby, all of them giving Lawless and Catarina sullen, hostile looks.

El Flaco did not rise on seeing them. Leaning back against the wall with a cigarillo drooping from his lips, he eyed Catarina with a mixture of anger and distrust as she and Lawless approached. When they stood before him, he ordered them to sit down and then indicated Delfina beside him.

'You owe your lives to the señora,' he said, speaking in Spanish. 'It was in my heart to shoot you both, but she has convinced me not to.'

'Glad to hear it,' Lawless said.

El Flaco ignored him and glared at Catarina. 'You, señorita, I especially wanted to kill.'

If she was frightened by his remark, typically she didn't show it.

'This man,' El Flaco continued, pointing at Lawless, 'is a *gringo*, so it is natural for him to lie and betray others. But you, woman, you are one of us, and I treated you with respect.'

Catarina spat defiantly on the ground. 'You hoped to get between my legs,' she said. 'This and nothing else was always on your mind. So let us not pretend or insult each other with lies, *jefe*. It only adds to our treachery.'

El Flaco's deep-set black eyes glittered with rage and his right hand strayed to his holstered pistol.

But before he could draw it, Delfina said quickly, 'I didn't come here to listen to your petty squabbles. So keep your *pistola* leathered, El Flaco. And you,' she added to Catarina, 'keep your mouth quiet or I will shoot you myself.'

Lawless saw the anger in her dark brown eyes and knew she meant it.

'Everybody, calm down,' he said. Then to El Flaco: 'Where is Señorita Albright?'

'I have sent for her.'

'Good. 'cause I've come to take her home.'

'You're not taking her anywhere,' a voice said. 'She's my wife and she stays where I tell her to stay.'

Lawless and the others turned toward the entrance as the Albrights entered. Though the light was dim, Lawless noticed the new bruise purpling Tess's cheek and automatically reached for his six-gun. His fingers found only the empty holster, and cursing silently, he rose and confronted Tucker Albright.

'That's where you're wrong, you gutless sonofabitch. Mrs. Albright is comin' back to New Mexico with me, an' I just hope you try to stop me, 'cause I'm goin' to enjoy beatin' you bloody.'

185

Despite being the larger of the two men Tucker stepped back, alarmed by Lawless's quiet seething rage; then, realizing he had belittled himself, he tried to stand tall and defiant in an attempt to reassert himself.

'A-Any time you w-want to try,' he blustered, 'I'm your man.'

Lawless, almost gleefully, started forward, fists clenched — but before he could reach Tucker, Delfina quickly stepped between them.

Confronting Tucker, she slapped him across the face.

'W-What the hell,' he began.

She slapped him again, so hard it echoed off the walls like a pistol shot.

'Damn you — ' he cursed.

She slapped him a third time. And as he staggered back, hands raised to defend himself, she drew her pistol and pressed the muzzle against his forehead, saying: 'It would give me great joy to shoot you, you *vil cobarde*, but my father sent me here to talk, not kill . . . But I warn you,' she said, holstering her gun, 'touch this woman again and I will order my men to bury you alive with the ants. Now,' she added, 'sit down and do not open your mouth again.'

Tucker stood there for an instant, desperately trying to find the guts to defy her. Then, true to form, he slunk away and sat with his back against the wall.

Delfina turned to Tess, her tone softening as she said: '*Mujer a mujer*, do you wish to stay here or return to your country?'

'She wants to go back to the States,' Lawless said.

'I am asking her, not you,' Delfina snapped. Then to Tess: 'Please, señora, answer me truthfully. I have much to accomplish here before I return to Chihuahua and you and your problems are interfering with my plans.'

Tess looked at her husband, who immediately turned away. Then she looked questioningly at Lawless, who met her leveled gaze.

'I wish to go home,' she said to Delfina. 'My marriage is over.'

'You can't be serious?' Tucker blurted. 'You love me too much to ever run out on me like this.'

Tess looked at her husband with something closer to pity than love. 'I'm not running out on you, Tuck. You've driven me away. There's a difference — even though I don't expect you to see it.'

'Please,' he begged. 'I'll never hit you again. I promise.' Then as she stood there, silent, wavering: 'If you love me, Tess, you'll stay.'

She didn't answer for a long moment. Then sadly, tears in her eyes, she said: 'I never thought I'd say this, Tuck. But I don't love you. Not anymore. You've beaten it all out of me.' Turning to Delfina, she added: 'I want to go.'

Delfina turned to El Flaco, saying: 'Is it agreed?'

'*Si*,' he replied grudgingly. ' — *con una condicion*.'

188

'Name it,' Tess replied.

'You do not speak of what you have seen or heard here,' put in Delfina before the bandit leader could reply. 'Is that clear?'

'Perfectly. You have my word on it.'

El Flaco leaned close to Tess, his tone threatening as he said: 'Do you know what a *lengua suelta* is, señora?'

She had to think a moment before answering. 'Uhm . . . a loose tongue?' Then: 'A person who talks too much?'

'*Si*. And do you know what I do with such a person?'

'Cut their tongue off I imagine.'

'*Muy despacio*,' he said. 'Little piece by little piece.'

'If you're trying to frighten me,' she said, after a quick look at Lawless, 'you don't have to. I'm already scared enough. I promise I won't say a word,' she added to Delfina. 'I mean, why would I? I live just across the border from you.'

Delfina nodded. Her flat-crowned hat hung down her back and out of habit, she smoothed her pulled-back black hair with the palm of one hand. 'I believe you, señora. As for you,' she said to Lawless: 'You will escort Señora Albright back to her ranch. This you will do as a favor for me.'

'As a favor,' he agreed. 'Oh, an' as a favor to me, Señora Vargas, you'll let Señorita Mateos come with us.'

'No,' El Flaco said harshly. 'Catarina stays. I am not finished with her.'

'Then I don't go,' Lawless said. 'Simple as that, *hombre*.'

There was a tense, grim silence. No one spoke or moved.

'You are not in a position to bargain,' Delfina told Lawless.

'That ain't the way I see it,' he said. 'Hell, I hold all the aces. Kill me an' my government will come after you with soldiers. Just as they will if you harm Mrs. Albright. We all know that. We also know you can't fight the U.S. and *Presidente* Diaz's army at the same time. You try and any hope of the revolt bein' successful, or your father becomin'

190

president would be over like that — '
He snapped his fingers. 'An' the
governor wouldn't like that, would he,
Delfina? And neither would you. Or
you,' he added to El Flaco. ''cause
without a revolution to write your name
in the history books, *amigo*, you're nothin'
but a petty little bandit who'll die unknown
facing a *rurales* firin' squad.'

El Flaco sucked his breath in, fury
narrowing his eyes into two black slits.
Rising, he drew his machete and
pressed the blade against Lawless's
throat.

'What happens to me will not matter
to you,' he hissed, 'because you will
already be dead.'

'Before you kill him, *jefe*,' Delfina
said quietly, 'I suggest you think about
what the *gringo* said. Your future — our
future — depends on it.'

Trembling with rage, the bandit
leader held the sharp blade against
Lawless's throat another moment, the
pressure enough to draw a thin trickle
of blood.

Lawless held his breath and for one infinitesimal moment his heart seemed to stop.

Then El Flaco grudgingly lowered his machete and Lawless breathed again.

'A wise choice,' Delfina said. She waited until El Flaco had stormed out of the cave, followed by his men, before saying to Lawless: 'You seem to enjoy tempting fate.'

'Yeah,' he admitted. 'It's a bad habit of mine.'

'One that could seriously shorten your life.'

'Not so long as you're lookin' out for me.'

She smiled coldly. 'Do not count on my help forever, *querida*. Even my generosity has its limits.'

'I'll remember that,' Lawless said, adding: 'Am I done here?'

Delfina nodded. 'You are free to go.'

'What about Catarina and Mrs. Albright?'

'Take them with you.'

'No!' Tucker jumped up, pulled a pearl-handled derringer from his pocket and aimed it at Lawless. 'My wife stays — '

He went to pull the trigger but before he could, Lawless grabbed Delfina's pistol and shot him in the chest.

Tucker staggered back against the wall, blood reddening his white shirt, the derringer falling from his limp fingers.

Tess gasped and ran to her husband, trying to support him as his legs buckled. But his weight was too much for her and he collapsed at her feet. She quickly knelt beside him, cradling his head as he fought to tell her something. But no words came out. He stared at her, his eyes wide open, and then his head slumped against her breast.

She said, 'No, oh no,' several times very softly.

But Tucker didn't hear her. He was already dead.

'You fool,' Delfina hissed at Lawless. 'Don't you see what you've done by killing this man?'

'Don't worry,' he said, handing the

pistol back to her. 'No one's goin' to blame you or Mexico for this. I'll take his body back to the States with us an' explain what happened.'

'If you do that, what will become of you?'

'Most likely nothin'. I'll tell the judge it was self-defense, an' there's this marshal I know in El Paso who'll vouch for me. I'll end up with a slap on the wrist at most.'

Delfina smiled, relieved. 'I am glad, *querida*. You have a promise to keep.'

'How could I forget?' he said wryly. 'I'll be thinkin' of you the whole time I'm escortin' these fine ladies back to New Mexico.'

It was not the smartest thing to say.

Delfina lost her smile and her petal-shaped lips tightened into a jealous, thin white line.

Realizing Lawless may have just shot himself in the foot, Catarina quickly came to his rescue.

'Do not worry, señora,' she told Delfina. 'Once we are across the border, I will make sure that this worthless *gringo* returns to you.'

'*Gracias*,' Delfina said. Then softly, so only Catarina heard: 'He is not much, I know, but he is mine.'

'That's obvious,' Catarina said. 'During the ride here he never stopped talking about you . . . and what you meant to him.'

Surprised, but pleased, Delfina looked at Lawless.

'Is this true?' she asked him.

'You heard the lady,' he said.

Delfina looked long and hard at him, searching for some hint of a lie, and then, when she couldn't find one, seemed satisfied.

'Go,' she told him. 'And be sure that Señora Albright gets home safely.'

'Got my word on it,' he said. 'See you in Chihuahua.'

Delfina nodded, but in her eyes there was still a hint of distrust, as if she couldn't quite convince herself that he was ever going to return to her.

Relieved, Lawless guided Catarina over

195

to where Tess was still knelt, sobbing, beside the body of her husband.

'Time to go, ma'am,' he said gently.

Tess angrily pushed him away.

'Mrs. Albright, please . . . '

Again, she pushed him away.

Catarina grasped his arm and pulled him aside. 'Let me help her,' she whispered. 'You go get our guns and the horses.'

'What about him?' Lawless said, indicating Tucker's corpse.

'I will have them bring his body outside. Now, go. You are only adding to the señora's pain.'

Sensing she was right, Lawless nodded and started away. But after only a few steps he stopped, turned and looked at her.

'Back there with El Flaco,' he said quietly. 'You handled yourself just fine.'

'For a woman?' she teased.

'For anyone.' Lawless smiled. 'Reckon your grandfather would've been real proud of you.' He turned away before she could thank him and left the cave.

23

They were a solemn little group.

With Lawless out front, leading the pack horse carrying Tucker's blanket-covered corpse, and Catarina and Tess riding side-by-side behind him, they rode in silence toward the mouth of the canyon.

Tess had stopped crying shortly after they'd left the bandits' camp. But her raw-eyed, tight-lipped expression clearly revealed the pain she was feeling.

At first Lawless had tried to console her. But when just the sight of him seemed to increase her suffering, it made him realize just how deeply she'd loved her husband — and though he couldn't figure out why a woman of her caliber could love a gutless bully like Tucker, he'd switched places with Catarina and taken over the lead.

They were almost out of the canyon

now. They rounded a bend in the steeply descending trail and there, a short distance ahead, was the entrance . . . and beyond, sprawled out below the green foothills, the vast sun-scorched desert leading to the border.

Lawless felt a sense of relief. Though Delfina had assured him they had nothing to fear from El Flaco or his men, Lawless remembered the hatred blazing in the bandit leader's eyes as he stormed out of the cave, and knew they wouldn't be completely safe until they'd crossed over into New Mexico.

But now, as they neared the entrance, under the ever-watchful eyes of the cliff-top lookouts, Lawless had to admit to himself that they probably had nothing to worry about.

Twisting around in the saddle, the sudden movement making the skittish stallion crab-step, Lawless looked at Catarina and mouthed: 'Everything okay?'

She nodded, pursed her lips and mischievously blew him a kiss.

He grinned and arched his eyebrows suggestively.

Catarina smiled — a playful, provocative smile that promised him she was his from now on.

It was an empty promise.

A single rifle shot rang out.

The bullet knocked Catarina from the saddle, ending her life.

Stunned, Lawless whirled back around and saw El Flaco and two of his men standing in the trail in front of him.

All had rifles. All were trained on Lawless.

El Flaco laughed contemptuously and started to mock Lawless.

It was his last mistake.

Lawless jerked his iron and fired so quickly, El Flaco's words died in his throat.

Slowly, he sank to his knees, staring in wide-eyed shock at Lawless. A moment later he pitched forward onto his face. Dead.

Lawless confronted the other two bandits.

Both dropped their rifles and fearfully raised their hands.

Lawless, too enraged to stop killing now, started to pull the trigger.

'No . . . '

In his fury Lawless barely heard Tess's cry and for a moment he could barely control his urge to shoot.

'Please — don't!'

This time the desperate pitch of her pleading brought him back from the brink.

He lowered his gun and looked around.

Tess had already dismounted and was now cradling Catarina's crumpled body against her.

'No more killing,' she begged. '*Please.*'

'What about her?' Lawless said, referring to Catarina. 'Doesn't she deserve somethin'?'

'A new life awaits her,' Tess said. 'As it does my husband. Don't stain it with more blood.'

Lawless fought down his rage, his urge to kill the bandits, and then looked up at the lookouts atop the sun-drenched cliffs.

'If you want to live,' he growled at the bandits, 'tell your friends to let us pass.'

One bandit removed his sombrero and waved it at the lookouts. As one, they lowered their rifles.

'It is safe for you now, *hombre*.'

'Better hope so,' Lawless said darkly. ''cause I'm prayin' for a reason to kill you.' Dismounting, he moved to Tess's side. 'I'll take her now,' he said, hunkering down.

Tess opened her arms, allowing Lawless to pick up the limp, bleeding body.

He straightened up, with her in his arms, and gently kissed Catarina.

Her lips were cold and lifeless, like those of a statue.

Lawless sighed and felt something joyful die inside him.

Carrying Catarina to her horse, he gently draped her over the saddle.

'She's got an uncle in Palomas,' he

told Tess. 'He'd want her to be buried near him.'

Tess didn't say anything. But the warm glow in her tear-filled eyes told him how sorry she was that Catarina was dead.

Helping her to get back on her horse, Lawless swung up into his own saddle and told the two bandits to start walking. They obeyed.

Lawless turned to Tess with new-found respect. If rage could blind him, he realized, could make him want to go on killing, it was possible that love could break her spirit — make her a human doormat for her husband's bullying. But now, free of him, perhaps she could regain her independence, the audacity that Lawless so admired. He surely hoped so.

'Ride alongside me, ma'am,' he told her gently. 'Maybe we can keep each other company.'

Tess managed a slight smile. 'I'd like that, Mr. Lawless.'

Together, they rode onward, Lawless

holding the reins of both the pack horse and Catarina's horse.

Shortly they were out of the canyon and descending into the foothills.

High above them buzzards circled lazily on the thermals.

Lawless looked back into the canyon a final time.

The buzzards came gracefully swooping down, wings flapping, legs extended . . . and landed beside El Flaco's blood-soaked body.

It wasn't much satisfaction, Lawless realized as he watched the big ugly birds tearing at the corpse with their beaks, but it was better than nothing.

THE END

THE OUTLAW'S DAUGHTER

C. J. Sommers

Matt Holiday is riding a dangerous
trail. With $20,000 in missing gold
to find and gunfighter Frank Waverly
searching for him, it seems unlikely
the gold will ever be returned to the
Butterfield Stage Company. And the
most dangerous gun on the range
belongs to the beautiful Serenity
Waverly, Frank's daughter. Although
she rides with Matt, he suspects that
will last only as long as it takes them
to recover the stolen gold . . .

IRON EYES THE FEARLESS

Rory Black

Iron Eyes has outgunned the Lucas gang but then discovers that the reward money may not be paid out. Downing most of a bottle of whiskey, Iron Eyes spots another outlaw in the saloon. With time to kill, he allows Joe Kane to run and then sets out after him into forested Indian territory, where he comes under attack. Wounded and tethered to a stake, as triumphant chants echo all around him, he awaits his fate silently. He is unafraid. He is Iron Eyes the Fearless.

GUNS FOR GONZALEZ

Corba Sunman

Captain Slade Moran is tracking three army deserters who have stolen guns and supplies to sell to Mexican bandit, Gonzalez. Time is against Moran, and his situation is about to get even more complicated. The daughter of Gonzalez, fleeing her father's anger, is being pursued by Gonzalez's men, and by breakaway rebel Pedro Sanchez, who wants to use her as a bartering chip against her father. And when the bullets start flying, Captain Moran is right in the middle . . .

RIDE THE SAVAGE RIVER

Scott Connor

Marshal Ellis Moore had been cleaning up Empire Falls for twelve years, but is killed taking on the last of the gun-toters who control his town. At the funeral, Moore's sons learn that he had been on the payroll of Samuel Holdstock, a notorious villain who is now spreading his corrupting influence downriver. Daniel and Henry vow to put right their father's mistakes and deliver Holdstock to justice — a mission even the formidable US Marshal Lincoln thinks is doomed to fail.